DEATH DROP

'There isn't a fag system, is there?'

'No'

'No organised bullying?'

'If there is it's undercover.'

The answer perturbed him. 'Who thumped him about the baseball?'

'A boy called Durrant.'

'How old?'

'Fifteen.'

'Three years older. Three years heavier. What did Hammond do about it?'

Some of her ash had fallen on her jeans. She brushed it off. 'He dealt with him suitably – whatever that means. He wouldn't allow Durrant to bully David.'

'Wouldn't he? He doesn't impre___ ___e as being competent.'

She s___ ___'re
begin___ ___ barrister.
It brea___ ___nd if I
though___ ___ then I
would ___ ___dent. It
can't po___ ___g else.'

**Also by the same author,
and available from Coronet Crime:**

TIME AND TIME AGAIN
DYING TO MEET YOU
NURSERY CRIMES
SEMINAR FOR MURDER
THE TWELFTH JUROR
VICTIMS

About the author

B.M. Gill's previous novels include THE
TWELFTH JUROR (winner of the Crime
Writers' Association Gold Dagger), VICTIMS,
SEMINAR FOR MURDER, DYING TO MEET
YOU and, most recently, TIME AND TIME
AGAIN. She lives in Anglesey.

Death Drop

_____

B. M. Gill

CORONET BOOKS
Hodder and Stoughton

First published in Great Britain in 1979 by Hodder and Stoughton Ltd

Coronet edition 1982

Coronet Crime edition 1990

British Library C.I.P.

Gill, B. M.
Death drop.—(Coronet Books)
I. Title
823'.914[F]   PR6057.1538

ISBN 0 340 28111 1

Printed and bound in Great Britain for Hodder and Stoughton paperbacks, a division of Hodder and Stoughton Ltd., Mill Road, Dunton Green, Sevenoaks, Kent TN13 2YA (Editorial Office: 47 Bedford Square, London WC1B 3DP) by Cox & Wyman Ltd., Reading.

One

THE MORTUARY WAS in the hospital grounds. Fleming had imagined a cement building lurking down one of Marristone's side streets. This place stood high on the Kent cliffs and had been weathered by salt winds. The smell — out here, at least — was the almond of gorse and the tang of seaweed. Gulls swooped in the breeze and the cold sun lay in splashes on his hands. He was perpetually cold as if he walked in heavy breakers through an icy sea. The coldness had started permeating him during the headmaster's long-distance phone call to the Bombay office. In the heat of an Indian afternoon it had crept through his pores with each word spoken.

"David has had an accident. A fall down the hold of a ship at the Maritime Museum."

"Dear sweet Christ! How badly hurt is he?"

A silence for a couple of minutes and then Brannigan's appalled voice had faltered on, "In all my time at Marristone Grange I've never before had to tell a parent that his son . . ." He hadn't been able to get it out. The death of a twelve-year-old was an obscenity.

Fleming had caught the first flight to England. Brannigan had met him at Heathrow and he had spent last night at the school house. Through a miasma of anger rather than grief — as yet the wound was too anaesthetised by shock for him to feel — he had listened to Brannigan's explanation. The boys had been in the care of Hammond, one of the housemasters. They were working on a project on maritime history and were given separate assignments on board ship. David's assignment had been on the poop deck. For some

5

reason best known to himself he had gone to the lower deck where the open hatch was. At this point Brannigan had looked away from him. "He had blindfolded himself — an imaginative twelve-year-old playing out an adventure film, perhaps. His hands were free. I have questioned everyone concerned very closely — there was no-one near him at the time."

Fleming, who had until then visualised a rubber-soled shoe slipping on a companionway, felt the new shock like a sword thrust in the gut. If negligence — or worse — could be proved, he had told Brannigan, he would take the school apart brick by brick.

Brannigan, grey-faced, had deferred argument. His tolerance and understanding coupled with Mrs. Brannigan's nervous and highly emotional hospitality were more than he could take. This morning, after one night at the school, he had arranged accommodation at The Lantern, one of the inns at Marristone Port. Brannigan's offer to accompany him to the mortuary he had crisply declined.

"Then let Dr. Preston go with you. It's too much of an ordeal to face on your own. I had arranged for the three of us to be there at eleven."

It was necessary to see the doctor. He had agreed to that.

It had already gone eleven. He began walking restlessly along the cliff path. The doctor was late. God damn them all in this place. And then he heard a car coming and retraced his steps.

There were two cars drawing up in the parking area by the mortuary. The first was a sleek, maroon Dolomite. The second a rusty black Morris Minor. Whoever was in it stayed in it. The owner of the Dolomite came to meet him — a big, balding man in a grey tweed suit.

He thrust out his hand. "Mr. Fleming? I'm sorry you had to wait. I assumed you'd be at the school house."

"Under the circumstances?"

"Both Brannigan and his wife are deeply distressed."

"Naturally . . . the reputation of the school . . ." It was vicious.

"That, too — but not just that. They're caring people. You malign them."

"Let's get on with it, shall we?"

Preston walked with him towards the mortuary. "There aren't any adequate phrases of sympathy. I'm sorry. We all are. The only consolation I can offer is that David died instantly and without pain. The fall broke his neck. I know that without a post-mortem, but the post-mortem will confirm it. I don't expect the pathologist to find anything else."

He pushed open the mortuary door and called out for Gamlin who was in the office off the main corridor. Gamlin, who had been smoking, stubbed his cigarette out on a tin lid that had once held adhesive tape.

Fleming smelt tobacco and formalin. The corridor was painted green and had a stone floor. Double doors with glass insets led off it into the main room. He had steeled himself to accept a clinical filing system of bodies in metal drawers, but if they were there they were tactfully out of view. In an alcove at the end of the room and partly hidden by a white screen was a hospital trolley. The small form on it was covered by a sheet. For a moment he stood in the middle of the room and couldn't move forward.

Preston said quietly, "You'll see him as you remember him — but take your time."

He began walking again. This time up to the trolley. The sheet was over David's face. He drew it back slowly. There were dark marks about the temples just below the springing fair hair. A small cut above the left eyebrow was a tiny line of mauve. Dark eyelashes lay thickly against the smooth freckled skin as if he slept. But this was no sleeping face.

This was nothing. Something loved. Something gone. David. Not here. Nowhere.

A shaft of sunlight came through the high window and lay across the trolley. It touched the skin with false colour as if nature tried to make amends.

Preston was at his side. "Did you want a priest? It didn't occur to me you might."

"No."

"Do you want to stay awhile? Gamlin will fetch you a chair."

"A few minutes — no chair — just leave me."

He stood emptily by the trolley. What words now, David? Your hand is a stiff ball of ice. I'm touching it. It's colder than mine.

I love you — wherever you are.

That goes on.

He turned at last and walked through what seemed a Siberian wilderness or non-reality towards the main door. There was a girl standing there — not looking at him — looking at David. She was carrying wild flowers — a rough posy of harebells and pinks. She was walking over to the trolley — standing there — putting the flowers on the white sheet — still standing there. Now walking away, her face awash with tears.

Outside he felt the bite of the wind and heard the distant roar of the sea. He went over to the sea-wall and tried to struggle back to some awareness of his own personal identity.

He turned and looked back at the mortuary. The doctor and the girl were standing by the door waiting for him — but giving him time. He went back to them. The girl, precariously calm, had stopped crying. Her lips were tight with tension and she avoided looking at him.

Preston introduced her. "This is Jenny Renshaw from the school. She's the matron and she knew David. She wants me

8

to apologise for the way she walked in — intruded on your grief. But she cared about him. And she had the flowers." He remembered Gamlin's furious expression. Wild flowers in a mortuary — petals on a corpse. He had steered her out before Gamlin's annoyance could explode into words. He added, smiling at her, "Her function is to be around. To drive you wherever you want to go."

She found her voice at last and the words came out thickly, "Or to leave you alone. If you can't stand being with anyone — then say so."

Her perceptiveness touched him so that he could almost feel human. The rejection that had begun to form in his mind became a reluctant acceptance. He didn't know he needed human companionship, but he was beginning to know it. She had wept for David. She was the first who had shown any genuine emotion for David.

There was a bond.

He thanked her briefly.

Preston told him that there was a form to sign concerning the autopsy which would take place the following day. They walked back to the hospital together while Jenny waited in the car.

He seemed to her like a man not fully alive — as if he walked and talked because his body was geared to walk and talk. An awareness of his death-wish pricked her into something deeper than pity.

When he returned she asked him where he wanted to be driven. Brannigan had told her to try to persuade him to return to the school, but she was wise enough not to try. The role of ambassadress had been thrust on her. In no way was she accountable for the accident. As the youngest and only non-teaching member of staff Fleming would scarcely rate her as an opponent. At best, Brannigan said, he might listen to her sort of reasoning — at worst he would dismiss her. There would be no overt animosity.

9

Fleming didn't know where he wanted to go. "Anywhere. Could you just drive for a while? Anywhere."

She understood that he didn't want to go directly to The Lantern. He didn't want to meet anyone and neither did she. The cliff road was fairly empty at this time of day. She drove fast and dangerously. When she was less emotional she slowed down.

He wasn't as she had expected him to be. He didn't look like David.

She halted the car on a farm track leading off the main road.

"He was like his mother, then?"

"Yes. Small-boned. Fair."

She wondered what words she could use to take the pain out of the silence and couldn't think of any. David's mother had died over a year ago. It had been less than tactful to mention her.

"Why did Brannigan send you?"

She nearly said, "To entice you back to the school," but stopped herself in time. "To provide transport until you make your own arrangements."

To put an electric fence around the tiger, she thought, and keep him safe from the local Press. There had been a staff meeting before morning school during which Hammond had been persuaded to take a day away from the premises. Brannigan had told him to steer clear of Fleming until Fleming was in a more rational frame of mind. "He's too shocked and grieved to make sound judgments. He's out for blood — mine — but yours, too, as you were in charge of the lads." Hammond had retorted explosively that his conscience was perfectly clear. "Agreed. You know it. I know it. In time Fleming will know it, too. Express your sympathy and make your explanations when he's ready to hear them. Not today."

They had gone on to talk about legal representation at the

inquest. There was to be a governors' meeting during which a plan of action would be drawn up. The school, already shaky in an economic climate that eroded its foundations, needed the strongest support it could get.

A hanging judge, Alison Brannigan, the head's wife, had described Fleming. Tread softly — softly.

A child is dead, Jenny had thought as she listened to them, and you're all so frightened of the consequences that you're getting your priorities wrong. And yet Brannigan himself had integrity and was compassionate. He didn't use the word pity, though. Perhaps the word was too mild.

She said roughly to Fleming, "David — his dying. It's such a waste."

There was a tremor in her voice again and he saw that she was clenching her jaw. He couldn't talk about it and looked away from her. There were sheep in the adjoining field. Wisps of wool had become entangled in a briar bush. Their bleating was a low accompaniment to the sound of the wind. The sea across the headland was getting rougher. It could be blowing up to a storm. It was mid-June and felt more like December. He was aware of everything in far-off, yet minute, detail as if he were an observer from a distance.

She said, "You're very cold, aren't you?"

"I suppose so. I've stopped noticing it."

"Are you ready to move on?"

"Where?"

"Somewhere where there isn't anyone — like this — only indoors with a fire going and some whisky."

"Your place?"

"My parents' flat in Nelson Street. They're away for a month in Spain. It's a bolt-hole from the school when I get time off."

He hesitated, but couldn't think of anywhere else to go. A bolt-hole from the school implied that she wasn't likely to put up an impassioned defence of the school. She might speak with some truth of it. Truth, as yet, was virgin ground.

The flat, high-ceilinged and shabbily elegant, was furnished with well-chosen Victoriana. The fire was already laid in the grey marble fireplace and she put her lighter to the slivers of wood. "Sit down over there near the heater. I'll switch it on until the fire burns up. Could you eat anything if I make you a meal?"

"No, not now — but you go ahead."

"I couldn't either — a drink, though, that's different."

She returned in about five minutes with a bottle of whisky and a jug of hot water.

"As you're so cold you'd be wise to take it hot — but I've ice if you'd prefer it that way." She took two tumblers out of the sideboard. "How do you want it?"

"Up to now I've been keeping myself sober."

"For God's sake, why?"

Because, he thought, I've been walking in enemy territory. Instinct told him that no longer applied — at least not here.

He took one of the tumblers and held it out to her. "I'll have it neat."

They drank in silence. Hers was well diluted. Each time she replenished his glass he made a token protest which she ignored. He didn't remember the point at which she got up and left the room. He didn't hear the front door closing behind her. When she returned towards the middle of the afternoon he was asleep on the sofa, his shoes kicked off, his tie loosened. There was a grimy swollen look about his face as if he had wept.

When Jenny hadn't returned to the school by three, Brannigan phoned the flat in Nelson Street. It seemed to him quite likely that Fleming had declined her company and gone for a long walk on his own. In similar circumstances he thought he would have done that himself. It was a long shot that they were in the flat together. He hoped she hadn't brought him home. It was thoughtless of her not to keep him informed.

Jenny heard the phone ringing and went into the hall and looked at it. It kept on ringing and she leaned against the wall with folded arms and made no move to answer it.

Fleming, forced into wakefulness by the bell, stumbled off the sofa and went into the hall. Answering phones was a conditioned reflex even when in a semi-stupefied state. For a moment or two he couldn't remember who Jenny was. A shaft of sunlight through the transom window above the door blazed like fire in her short red hair. She moved out of its beam.

The phone stopped.

"You didn't answer it."

She shrugged. "It was probably a recall to duty."

"Duty?" He was still very unclear about everything.

"School."

He remembered. The pain had a different quality now. The numbness had become a dull ache. He was no longer cold. The room had become uncomfortably hot and his body felt sticky with sweat. He had drunk too much — or perhaps not enough.

She smiled at him. "The bathroom is the second door on the right. Have a shower while I brew up some black coffee. Later, there's some braising steak doing quietly in the cooker."

"You're being very kind." The words came out automatically, but he meant them. Each moment lived in this, the most terrible period in his life, had been made almost bearable by her care.

When he returned to the sitting room he felt fresher and able to form the words with some clarity.

"Did David ever talk about me — to you?"

She couldn't with honesty remember. "David talked about times and places. You lived in Oxford. I think?"

"Yes, briefly. And then we moved to Stroud in Gloucestershire."

"A cottage on the edge of the Cotswolds?"

"Yes, that's it." He took the coffee from her and declined sugar. "He described that to you?"

"Not exactly." She tried to find the right words. "A kids' party. Balloons. Only not a kids' party — balloons — just that sort of feeling about a place. The way he looked when he spoke. It was the way he looked, not the words."

"Super."

"What? Yes. But then they all say that."

"Did David say anything to you that you particularly remember?"

She gave the question some thought before replying. "He'd come into the infirmary sometimes — with one excuse or another — and if there wasn't anyone else there he'd chat about this and that. Nothing I particularly remember."

"Did he ever talk about his mother?"

"Only in the same way that you and she were part of the same time — the old days, he used to say, as if he were Methusalah."

The old days. Ruth. During the time in Gloucestershire she had been well. The marriage had been strong then, too, slipping a little perhaps, but not perceptibly.

"Did he ever mention London?"

"He said you had a flat in London — that he went there with you for holidays — when he wasn't travelling around with you. You took him to some exotic places."

"Only in the line of business — selling electronic equipment to a worldwide market. He did a lot of waiting around. Measles once in a hotel in Florence . . . Did he mention that?"

"No. I think he was selective. He remembered the good things. Who chose Marristone Grange for him?"

"His mother — during the last few months of her illness. Her brothers went to Marristone. In those days, I gather, it flourished. At any rate they survived." It was bitter.

She contemplated him silently. Waiting for it.

It came. "Tell me about Marristone — Marristone today."

A vision of Brannigan rose up to haunt her. "What do you want to know?"

"Everything I don't already know. When I went to see it, it seemed to be adequate. The age range was wide. It catered for single parent families insofar that it didn't close down at holiday time. David was too old for prep school and he didn't have his name down for any of the better public schools. Ruth's brothers had done well there academically. The fact that the school is smaller now seemed a point in its favour. It was a convenient solution to a difficult problem. Obviously I didn't look deeply enough. David seemed happy. He didn't complain. Was there reason for complaint?"

She didn't answer straight away but got up and lit herself a cigarette and then offered the box to him. He shook his head.

Did ebullient children grow into quiet children? she wondered. The infirmary had been sanctuary for David — but not only for David. A quiet room — a little mothering. Was he any different from the rest? That look about the eyes — some of the others had it, too, the introspective ones. The only time he had been with her for a longish period was recently when he had mumps. And that had been a genuine physical illness. At the end of it some of the old ebullience had bubbled up again, until the very last day when he was due back in the main school. But the infirmary was a holiday — no child liked work. They all reacted in the same way — well, perhaps not in quite the same way. He had become white and very withdrawn. Reason for complaint?

She drew on her cigarette. "Children endure boarding-school. It isn't a natural way of life. Some of them endure it better than others. When the young ones come — the seven- and eight-year-olds — they cry. If the housemaster's wife is any good at her job she mops them up and pets them a bit and makes them feel better. When they're David's age — eleven going on twelve — they don't cry. They put up with it. They make themselves as tough as their nature lets them. When they're older than that they start to get important — they boss the other kids around — they're part of the hierarchy then, the upper part. When the time comes to leave they say 'Good old Marristone, wouldn't have missed it for the world'."

"You haven't answered me. We're talking about David, not the children in general."

She sighed. "I know. I don't think I can answer you. If I had taught him every day in class I might be able to answer you. I'm a matron. My duties are limited. I saw David when he was sick with mumps and I patched him up once or twice after rugger." She hesitated. "And once after a fight about rugger. He'd been to the States with you and told one of the boys that baseball was better. The boy thumped him. I thought he'd thumped him too hard and I told Brannigan. Brannigan said it was too trivial to report to him — that I should have told Hammond, David's housemaster."

Brannigan, Fleming thought, was probably right. David had been thumped in his other schools for one reason or another and had done some thumping back.

"There isn't a fag system, is there?"

"No."

"No organised bullying?"

"If there is it's undercover."

The answer perturbed him. "Who thumped him about the baseball?"

"A boy called Durrant."

"How old?"

"Fifteen."

"Three years older. Three years heavier. What did Hammond do about it?"

Some of her ash had fallen on her jeans. She brushed it off. "He dealt with him suitably — whatever that means. He wouldn't allow Durrant to bully David."

"Wouldn't he? He doesn't impress me as being competent."

She spoke with some sharpness. "You're beginning to sound like a prosecuting barrister. It breaks my heart that David is dead and if I thought there was any fault anywhere then I'd say so. He fell. It was an accident. It can't possibly be anything else. You've got to believe that or you'll drive yourself crazy."

"Then you'd say he was happy in school?"

"As happy as any of them. You know how it is."

Her words had consoled him a little and some of his own guilt went. It might have happened in any other school. It might have happened anywhere.

It was while they were eating the steak some while later that Jenny remembered the sketch. David had drawn it for her while he was convalescing from the mumps. He had been sitting near the window with the sketching block on his knees. It had taken him about half an hour to do it. He had handed it to her without a word, watching her face for a reaction. She had quite spontaneously laughed and been surprised that he hadn't laughed with her. It had seemed to her a funny drawing. She had kept it in case he asked for it back. Boys — especially the younger ones — tended to test her loyalty by asking her if she still had whatever treasure they had bestowed on her. Treasures included conkers, a

17

rat's tail, a magnet, love poems. They all went into a duffel bag and remained there for a safe period. The duffel bag was in the kitchen drawer. She fetched it. The drawing was creased and grubby and she touched it for a moment with tenderness before handing it over. "Something David drew for me when he had mumps."

Fleming took the folded drawing from her, opened it up, and put it on the table.

"Good Christ Almighty!" He sat rigid, fighting nausea.

She was astonished by his reaction, alarmed at his pallor. "It's a joke drawing. He gave it to me dead-pan. Just fun."

He didn't hear her. He was six years back in time. Ruth and he returning at one-thirty in the morning after the car had broken down on a deserted country road. The holiday cottage in darkness. David screaming. The babysitter had left at midnight. He had woken in the dark alone. The tiger moth caterpillar had dropped on his pillow from a bowl of flowers near the bed. He had wakened to feel its slow furry crawl across his cheek. A strange inimical room — silence — and an appalling creature on which to vent his terror.

There had followed two years of nightmares in which the caterpillar, man-sized, was the beast. On each day that followed a disturbed night he drew the caterpillar and then hid the drawing, but in obvious places where it could be found. He and Ruth had made a point of finding the drawings and tearing them up. It had become a ritual. He watched whilst appearing not to watch. In time the drawings and the nightmares stopped. There hadn't been a nightmare or a drawing for four years.

Until this drawing now.

A crude, immature, thickly shaded, heavily furred caterpillar, hugely out of proportion, sprawling over a small bed. At the bottom of the picture in big uncontrolled six-year-old letters: WOLLY BEAR ON D'S BED.

Woolly Bear had been Ruth's name for it when she had

picked it off his face. Woolly Bear. Wolly as the six-year-old David had spelt it. Wolly as the twelve-year-old David had spelt it now.

Two

"MAY I HAVE permission to go into Marristone Port, sir?"

Brannigan looked in some irritation at Durrant who had knocked at his study door and been told brusquely to enter. He didn't like the boy and tended to over-react in his favour in an effort to appease his conscience. Any other boy he would have told sharply to take his request to the appropriate quarter and not presume to waste his time. He said much the same thing to Durrant but with more restraint.

"You know the procedure, Durrant. If you need to go into Marristone Port for any reason, you ask your house-master."

Durrant licked his thick lower lip. "I can't find Mr. Hammond, sir. I don't think he's on the premises."

Brannigan glanced at his watch. It had just gone four. Hammond wouldn't be back, if he had any sense, until a lot later. He had forgotten momentarily that Durrant was in Hammond's House.

"Why do you want to go into Marristone Port?"

"It's my mother's birthday, sir. I want to get her a card and a present."

Brannigan wondered if it were a variation of the grand-mother's funeral theme and decided it wasn't. Durrant's mother didn't give a tuppeny damn for Durrant, but Durrant cared quite deeply for her. During his first year at

the Grange he had found his way home twice. The first time
to an empty house and he had walked the night streets of
Leeds until the police had picked him up. The second time
to a house which had been far from empty. His mother had
returned him personally the following day. Her anger had
been greater than her discretion and it hadn't been difficult
to imagine what the boy had walked in on. After that he had
stayed put. Whatever illusions he had left he clung to. His
father, with less tenacity, had long since ditched his and
taken himself off. He wrote to the boy once or twice a term
and the boy wrote a duty letter back. Their relationship was
polite and distant.

"When is your mother's birthday, Durrant?"

"Tomorrow, sir."

Brannigan felt the boy's anxiety coming across the room
in almost tangible waves. He was expecting to have his
request refused. He had probably spent a lot of time in a
fruitless search for Hammond and in desperation had come
at last to him. The shops closed at six.

He tried to remember Durrant's christian name and at
last it came to him. "Unless you're a lightning shopper,
Steven, you're likely to miss the post."

"I have my bike, sir. It won't take me long to get into
Marristone Port and I know what I want to buy."

"Something you can parcel up quickly?"

Durrant's stoop became almost more pronounced. He
was five foot eleven when he stood straight, but in moments
of embarrassment lost several inches. "A book of Keats'
poems, sir." It came out as a mumble.

Brannigan looked down at the blotter on his desk and
positioned it more centrally. When he looked up his face was
expressionless, amusement quenched.

"Mr. Hammond normally acts as banker for the House.
As he's not around what are you using for cash?"

Durrant shuffled his feet. "I was wondering if you could

spare the time to come across to the House office, sir, and get me five pounds from my account?"

Brannigan took out his wallet. "No, I haven't time. You can return this later when you've seen Mr. Hammond." He took out a five-pound note. "Is it a small book?"

"Yes, quite light, sir."

Brannigan took out an extra pound. "If you have any change — and any time — go to the chemist and get yourself a razor . . . or have you already got one?"

Durrant pocketed the money. "Thank you, sir. No, sir."

Brannigan's smile, though forced, came out with a little warmth. "You haven't a full-blown moustache yet, but it's coming along. You know the rules about that, Steven."

"Yes, sir."

"Then see to it."

As Durrant turned to go he called after him. "At fifteen you're old enough to go into Marristone Port without a prefect, and you're old enough to ride that bike of yours with due care and attention. Just a warning."

"Yes, sir."

"Well, go on then, or you'll miss the shops."

And for God's sake heed the warning, Brannigan thought. It would have been easy to have refused permission, but he couldn't wrap the boys up in cotton wool and shield them from all possible hazards. It was high summer now and light until well on into the evening. The roads were reasonably quiet. There was a slight thickening of the traffic between five and six, but no real rush hour. If Durrant finished up under a bus it would be one chance in an imponderable number of chances. The odds had been the same with young Fleming. The pall of anxiety that had oppressed him since the accident settled more heavily on him.

Once off the school premises Durrant rode his bike with panache. He had no illusions at all about Brannigan's apparent friendliness towards him. He didn't like him either. He saw him as commandant of Colditz and had several enjoyable fantasies in which he, Durrant, in the role of a British officer, led an uprising against him and had him hanged, shot, or less often poisoned. Poisoning lacked drama, but it was a variation of a theme. His fantasies about his mother's lovers were more up-to-date. They were vague shadow figures not fully known and not understood. He saw them as space creatures emerging from some far nebulae — creatures of doom — to be contained and liquidated in vast chemical vats or electrocuted into oblivion.

Now, as he rode his bike towards Marristone Port, he was at the controls of an interplanetary space machine. The glimpses of the coast as the road wound downhill towards the town were Martian scenes hazed over with red. The occasional glitter of the sea was the shine of enemy space craft approaching faster than light. The overtaking cars were capsules under his control and sent on as an advance combat force. Oncoming traffic was so much debris in space to be carefully avoided.

He looked briefly at Jenny's car as she drove it up the hill towards the school, but it didn't register in his mind as a car driven by Jenny. She raised her hand in greeting, but he stared blankly and pedalled on.

Unfriendly little beast, Jenny thought. She was glad Fleming wasn't in the car with her. After seeing the sketch all his prejudices against the school had become stronger than ever. He had phoned Brannigan requesting an inter-view just as soon as Brannigan could make it. Brannigan had suggested six o'clock. It was policy that Jenny should return on her own and that he should follow in a couple of hours in a taxi. On parting he had made it plain that he wanted to see her again. "You're the only person in the whole goddamned set-up who meant anything to David."

"I wouldn't say that. You can't write off all the staff like that. They're ordinary caring people."

"Then why the hell didn't they see what was happening to him?"

"But you can't be sure what was happening to him . . . this sketch . . ."

He interrupted her. "Shows six years' regression — what sort of mental agony brought that about?"

She was silent. If he were right then she would fight his battle with him, and resign from the school if that was the only way to do it. In the meantime she had to keep everything balanced and await events. Brannigan couldn't very well sack her for giving him the sketch in the first place, but he wouldn't exactly commend her for discretion. Had she known the sketch would have upset him so much she might well have withheld it. David was dead, what good did it do? But if she had withheld it, it would have been to spare him pain, not to have glossed things over for the school. One David had died. There were other Davids.

She parked the car in the parking space next to Hammond's which was still empty. She wondered where he had gone to and couldn't help feeling sympathy for him. He was a competent teacher — or so the others said, she didn't know much about the academic side of the school — and though he was a strict disciplinarian he was more tolerant in his attitude to the boys than some of the others. The word 'kind' summed him up as well as any other.

She tapped at Brannigan's door and he rose as she came in and drew out a chair for her.

"I'm sorry I was away so long." It was expected of her and had to be said.

"Not at all." He decided not to mention the phone call. "There's no limit on that sort of thing. Did you go into the mortuary with him?"

She found it very hard to speak about. There was a thickening in her throat again. "Yes."

He was aware of her distress and wondered just

how bloody-mindedly Fleming had behaved towards her.

"Was it very difficult?"

"You mean distressing — yes."

He accepted the rebuke. There had been some sort of rapport between them. "He didn't mind your being there?"

"At the mortuary? He was scarcely aware of me. Sam Preston introduced me afterwards. I told him I'd drive him anywhere he wanted to go."

"And he agreed to that?"

"He hadn't a car of his own."

He wished she would be more forthcoming. He didn't want the interview to sound like an inquisition. "And where did he want to go?"

"Just driving around. We went up on the coast road. He wanted time to be quiet."

"Did he talk to you about David — about the school?"

"He had just seen David. He was very shaken and upset. I had nursed David through mumps. I was — fond — of him. He sensed that. It helped."

"I see," Brannigan relaxed slightly. Jenny had been a wise choice. He tried to sum it up, "He accepted that you were well disposed to David and he therefore accepted you — would that be the situation?"

"Yes."

"So he was able to talk to you without rancour?"

"Yes."

"To what extent does he blame the school?"

Jenny said sharply, "I wasn't on reconnaissance in enemy lines, Mr. Brannigan. I'm sorry. I don't know."

Brannigan understood her distress and quenched his own flare of annoyance. She was young. She had been exposed to an emotional barrage. He would find out soon enough from Fleming how much he blamed the school.

Fleming's taxi drew up at the school house a few minutes

before six. Brannigan came out to meet him as he paid off the driver.

"Did you get fixed up at The Lantern — or didn't it come up to your expectations? You're welcome to stay here with us as long as you wish."

"Thank you, but The Lantern is perfectly adequate." He had returned there after leaving Jenny. A reporter had way-laid him in the hall and he had given him short shrift. He might have a story for the paper later, he had told him brusquely, but until he had all the facts he had nothing to say.

The polite preliminaries over, Brannigan asked him if he would like to come into the school house for a drink, or would he prefer to go over to his study in the main building.

"Your study. This is not a social call."

"But I can persuade you to stay for dinner? My wife will be most disappointed if you don't."

"I'm sorry. No."

Brannigan imagined Alison's sigh of relief. So the gloves were still off. At least he would keep his own on as long as possible. There was nothing to be gained by belligerence.

The walk to the main building was past the playing fields and the tennis courts. Four of the senior boys were having a game on the court near the shrubbery and a couple of the younger boys were acting as ball boys.

Brannigan went over to the wire netting enclosure and called one of the older boys to him. "Have Eldridge and Macey permission to be out of prep?"

Lambton rubbed a sweaty hand across his forehead. "Yes, sir. They finished early, sir."

"And they're doing this voluntarily?"

"Oh yes, sir. Of course, sir."

Brannigan snapped, "It seems a singular waste of their time. It would be far more useful if you gave them some coaching in the game. But I suppose you intend to do that anyway." It was a command.

"Yes, sir. As soon as we've finished this set, sir."

"Which will be soon, I hope?"

"After two games, sir."

Brannigan turned back to Fleming. At any other time he doubted if he would have interfered. He felt very much on the defensive and a slow anger burned in him. He had run this school for a number of years and he believed he had run it well. If the economic recession was killing it, then he was not to blame. Neither was he to blame for the death of this man's son. If Fleming was determined to pin the guilt on him, he was not going to stand quietly to attention and let him get on with it. Last night on the drive back from Heathrow to the school he had been strongly aware of Fleming's pain and had tried to give him what support he could, but Fleming's wall of animosity had separated them and grown higher as the night wore on.

He said, "I phoned The Lantern this morning — about the time I expected you to have returned from the mortuary. I wanted to express my sympathy."

"Thank you." It was cold.

"I was told there was a reporter there."

"I got rid of him."

"I'm sorry he bothered you."

"He didn't. I told him there was no story until I had my facts. That's why I'm here now."

Brannigan took him through the main hall and into his study. The room, despite its red carpet and curtains, looked austere and felt cold. There were photographs of each school year since nineteen-fifty-seven on the walls. The fact that the school numbers had shrunk considerably was apparent by the size of the frames.

Brannigan took the chair behind the desk, hesitated and then got up again and went to sit on one of the leather chairs by the empty fireplace. He indicated the other leather chair facing him.

"Before we start, is there anything I can get you to drink? Scotch, perhaps?"

"No, thank you." It was enemy territory again.

Brannigan decided to take the initiative. "I've made, and naturally will continue to make, every allowance for your distress, but I'm quite sure that the school is blameless. If you think differently now is the time to thrash the matter out. Ask me any questions you like. I'll answer you honestly and help in any way I can to put your mind at rest."

Fleming said crisply, "I have a lot of questions to ask you, but first of all I want to see David's work. You've kept his exercise books, I suppose?"

Brannigan let his astonishment show. In the present circumstances it was the last request he would have expected.

"Yes, of course I have all his books." The boy's clothes and possessions were packed in his school trunk, but the contents of his desk had been put in a large cardboard folder and locked in the safe. He went to fetch the folder and took it over to his desk. "I suggest you sit over here if you want to go through them."

Fleming took the folder and opened it slowly. The school exercise books were green with the crest stamped on the cover. Under the crest of the first book he removed was neatly written in David's small rather angular writing: *David John Fleming*, *Hammond's House*, *Class 4A History*. He opened it, but made no attempt to read what he saw. This was David alive, not David dead in the mortuary. His hand on the written page was touching David's warm, grubby, impatient hand. David John Fleming — not just a name, but David's voice naming his name. A lively voice with some of Ruth's north country accent in it. He had a strong memory of David's arms around his neck as they had embraced in the car before he had left him at the station to catch the school train. A private embrace before the public handshake on the platform. Very reserved in company, very

British stiff upper lip. A quiet "Good-bye, kiddo, I'll be thinking of you." An equally quiet "Telepathic message at nine o'clock spot on saying good night. Okay?" "Okay." Then aloud, laconically. "Be seeing you, Dad." "So long, David. Letters from India this time." "Super!" Eyes too bright, but the word coming out without a tremor. "Super!"

A traitorous wave of emotion took Fleming unexpectedly and for a moment he couldn't hide it. Brannigan noticed the clenched muscles of his jaw before he turned his head away.

It was several minutes before he was able to return to the folder.

The next three books were on mathematics. They contained average problems set a twelve-year-old and were reasonably handled. The book of essays he wanted to take away with him and read in private. He didn't feel he could trust himself to read them in Brannigan's presence. They were the essence of David. Sentences — echoes of David's voice — whispered up from the page before he could close his eyes and mind to them. "My first jumbo jet flight was with my Dad to New York. There was a film show — a Western — not very good. For lunch we had samon and lettice in boxes with plastic knives and forks. A woman in the next seat was sick in a brown paper bag and I couldn't eat any more lunch after that." Dad had been scored out with a red pen and Father put in instead. Samon had been corrected, but lettice had got through.

And further on: "The best pet I ever had was a gerbil. I had it when we had a house with a long garden in the Cotswolds. It lived in a shed in the orchard. It was a long time ago when I was young. My mother didn't like it, but she didn't say she didn't like it because she knew I did. It got lost under the floorboards once but my Father found it with a torch. My mother said she was glad it had been found. That was not honest, but it was kind." Fleming turned back a page and saw that the essay was headed *Honesty*.

He closed the book and put it on one side.

Honesty. "How are things with you at school, David?"

"All right, Dad."

"Any problems?"

"No — not really."

"You'd tell me if there were?"

"Yes, of course."

Had the inflection been right? Had he listened hard enough to find a note of doubt, of false brightness? Had he just hoped everything was all right and been too quick to accept David's word for it?

Surely he had known his own son well enough to be aware that he was putting on one hell of a cover-up.

As he must have been.

But these books were normal.

Inside the main folder was another smaller one with the words *Project on Maritime History* written carefully across it. There were drawings of Aegean Bronze Age vessels and Phoenician biremes. Then came a drawing on graph paper showing the measurements of a Viking ship. He had been given high marks for these and the written comment in red ballpoint: *Good. You have done your research well.*

He turned to Brannigan. "How many times did David go to the Maritime Museum?"

Brannigan noted that he had himself well in hand again. His voice was toneless and his eyes showed nothing.

"The boys were taken on a preliminary visit before each section was written about. The section on cargo vessels was the fourth."

"So it was on his fourth visit that he was killed?"

"Yes."

Fleming closed the folder and then ran his fingers up and down the edges of it as if he were loath to part with anything that David had touched. At last he pushed it aside.

"How would you rate his work?"

Brannigan answered honestly. "Average. He could do very well indeed if he set his mind on it."

"And you would expect this sort of work from a twelve-year-old?"

"Yes. As I told you, he was average. Not brilliant — just a good, steady, middle-of-the-road ability. The sort that sometimes surges ahead in early adolescence."

"Not the sort that drops back six years and regresses to the intellect of a child of six?"

Brannigan was startled. "I don't understand you."

Fleming took the sketch out of his wallet and handed it to him without a word.

Brannigan looked at the drawing of the caterpillar and the unformed writing under it. WOLLY BEAR ON D'S BED.

"What is this supposed to be? Some of David's early work from his kindergarten?"

"Some of David's most recent work — during his period in the infirmary when he had mumps."

"I don't believe it!" It came out explosively. What Brannigan saw as an attack from a totally unexpected quarter not only unnerved but astonished him. What the hell was Fleming playing at? This sketch he was holding was the work of an infant. It bore absolutely no resemblance to the books on the desk. And what was that about regression? To this? Fleming must be out of his mind if he thought he could con him that easily.

He handed it back. "You've kept this a long time."

"I've kept it a matter of hours. I saw it for the first time this afternoon. David drew it for Jenny a week or so ago on his last day in the infirmary. Jenny gave it to me."

Brannigan felt the blood thrumming in his head. He saw a whole kaleidoscope of possibilities including one in which Jenny was in collusion with Fleming to the tune of whatever damages they managed to milk from the school. And then

30

he became calm again and dismissed them. He didn't understand and until he did understand he would try and keep an open mind.

He asked Fleming to explain the significance of the drawing and listened without interrupting while he did so.

"And he hadn't drawn the caterpillar since he was — how old?"

"I think the last nightmare-linked drawing was when he was seven and a half going on eight."

"You took him to a psychiatrist?"

"No. We — his mother and I — tore up the drawings. We sensed that was what he wanted and it worked."

"You think he suffered some shock that pushed him back into this?"

"Shock. Or a long period of unhappiness. I don't know. That's what I mean to find out."

"And you believe that the state of his mind was disturbed — perhaps to the extent that the fall into the hold was suicidal — is that what you're saying?"

"I think it's possible. And if it's proved true then God help you, the school, and everyone in it."

Brannigan was suddenly aware of the coldness of the room. He repressed a shiver. The isolation of command was like a cloak of ice on his shoulders. His own conscience in the matter was clear, but ultimately he was answerable for his staff and the boys.

"A little teasing — a caterpillar in David's bed — that's the easy and most likely explanation." He managed to say it quite smoothly, almost persuasively.

"The caterpillar was linked with the terror of waking alone in a dark unfamiliar house — it's a symptom, not the disease."

"And what do you believe the disease is in this particular instance?"

31

Fleming answered flatly, "A prolonged period of bullying — perhaps sexual assault."

He had expected Brannigan to flare up into a quick denial, but his answer when it came was measured and thoughtful. "The two old bogies of the system. It would be naive of me to discount either possibility. I'm prepared to investigate both. But unless either is proved you'd be wise to say nothing to anyone."

"I shall say nothing provided the investigation is carried out without bias. I want to be around to see that it is."

Brannigan stood up. "Very well, Mr. Fleming. You shall be around. It's my school and your child. There is common ground for concern."

Three

JENNY WAS IN the staffroom watching a film on television when Brannigan and Fleming came in. She could tell by their faces that the interview hadn't been a quiet pussyfooting over delicate areas of dissent. Swords had been out on both sides. If they were sheathed now it was an uneasy truce.

Brannigan, relieved that Jenny was alone in the room, indicated the television. She went over and switched it off.

"You've come to ask me about the sketch." Characteristically she plunged straight in. She wondered if Fleming would stay around to pick up the pieces. His eyes had warmed as their glances met, but now he was standing with his back to the window watching her and saying nothing.

Brannigan sat on the arm of the nearest chair. He felt

extremely tired as if he were battling through a force eight gale.

"Yes — three questions. Did you actually see David drawing the caterpillar?"

"Yes, in the infirmary — on the day he was due to go back into the main school. One day last week."

"Did he have a shocking or frightening experience just before he drew it?"

"No. To my almost certain knowledge — no. He was a bit quiet on the last day — but none of the boys like getting back to work. I thought he did the drawing — just a fun thing — to cheer himself up."

"Why didn't you bring the drawing straight to me?"

She smiled slightly. "Together with the rat's tail and the conkers and Milford Minor's valentine? Do you seriously expect me to gather up all the boys' offerings and pass them on to you?"

Jenny's forthrightness occasionally sailed rather close to insolence, but Brannigan let it pass. "You regarded it with sufficient seriousness to give it to David's father."

"Had it been any other item in my duffel bag given me by David I would have given it to his father. It happened to be a sketch of a caterpillar."

"You couldn't tell by the nature of the drawing and the writing that the child was seriously disturbed?"

"No, I couldn't. It was a babyish drawing and babyish writing. I thought he'd done it that way for fun."

Brannigan looked at Fleming. "Have you anything to ask Nurse Renshaw yourself?"

There was one question he hadn't thought of asking her earlier. "Had you any other patients at that particular time — anyone who could have got at David and worried him in some way?"

"Three other boys had mumps. Two were the Rillman twins and the other was Peter Sellick."

Brannigan said, "Seven-year-olds. Not averse to putting a caterpillar in a bed — but nothing more sinister."

He suggested that Fleming should go along to see Mrs. Robbins. "She's a housemother for want of a better word. Her flat is near the Hammond House dormitory." It was policy that all housemasters should be married, but when Hammond's wife had left him at the end of the autumn term he could hardly request Hammond to leave too. Mrs. Robbins, a widowed sister of Laxby, the music master, was standing in temporarily. Dwindling numbers had made it possible to convert two small dormitories into a self-contained unit for her.

He asked Jenny if she were in.

"She was watching the early news here. She left when the film started. She isn't due to see the boys to bed until later, but she wouldn't have time to leave the premises."

Mollie Robbins didn't hear Brannigan's knock on her door. She was listening through her headphones to Schoenberg's *Pierrot Lunaire*. It was a recording that Laxby had given her and he had promised to come around later that evening to discuss Schoenberg's twelve-note theory. She had been researching the music of the Second Viennese School and hoped to get some facts down on her typewriter just as soon as she had seen the little horrors to bed.

Fleming's first impression of her, when Brannigan after his second unanswered knock opened the door, was of a huge blousy woman in headphones who looked at them with a dazedly beatific expression which quickly turned to annoyance. She switched off the recording and removed the headphones.

Brannigan introduced Fleming.

The last hazy notes of the music drifted from her memory as she looked at him. She saw a tall, gaunt, tired-looking man who was looking back at her as if he were trying to probe the recesses of her mind.

34

She looked away nervously. The disruption of her musical interlude was annoyance enough — God knew she needed the refreshment of it if she were to carry on her duties — without having to put up with what threatened to be a distressing and embarrassing interview with the dead child's father.

Brannigan asked if they might sit down.

"Of course." She uttered a few polite words of sympathy to Fleming which he acknowledged with a slight nod of the head.

Physically she appalled him. He tried to resist forming a prejudice. How she looked didn't matter.

Brannigan had sketched in a brief outline of her duties on the walk over to her flat and he left it now to Fleming to take the initiative.

"Mr. Fleming wants to ask you some questions about David. He understands about your dormitory duties and so on. Answer him as fully as you can."

"Of course." She folded her hands in her lap, uncomfortably aware of her bitten nails. Resentment burned in her. This was her own time. One of her escape periods into a world made civilised by music. In her young days she had hoped to become a concert pianist. A severed nerve in her right hand had put paid to that. What did he think she was — a lump of lard? An intellectual moron with rampaging flesh? Had he ever felt his spirit dance and laugh with Rossini? Did he think she was physically locked inside herself with an immovable ball and chain?

Their eyes met and held.

Fleming, aware of an antagonism equal to his own, knew he would have to soften her defences if he were to make any headway with her at all.

"As housemother you've probably formed quite a close relationship with the boys. If they were troubled by anything they would come to you?"

She was not to be quickly mollified. "Housemothers function in orphanages and approved schools. Here, the housemaster's wife is referred to as Mrs. whatever it is. I came to stand in for Mrs. Hammond when she left. The boys call me Mrs. Robbins to my face and Mary Lou behind my back."

Fleming wondered if Mrs. Hammond were away permanently and, if so, why. It couldn't at this stage be asked.

He achieved a bleak smile. "A nickname can be a sign of affection."

"All the staff have nicknames. In my case it's to rhyme with a line of doggerel — not particularly affectionate."

Fleming stopped trying to win her. "So — if there was any trouble the boys would cope as best they could themselves."

She caught a glimpse of Brannigan's expression out of the corner of her eye and knew she had to stop hazarding her position. Truth was a luxury she couldn't afford.

She climbed down. "No — they'd bring their troubles to me — naturally — and I'd do my best to help. Are you trying to tell me that something was troubling David?"

He acknowledged the breach in her armour but felt that it had been made too quickly. Her antagonism had been honest. She had switched it off like a light.

"I think he might have been having nightmares. Would you have been aware of it if he had been?"

She looked at him blandly. "The dormitory is just down the corridor. I very rarely go out of an evening. Of course I would have been aware of it."

Fleming looked at the hi-fi equipment and the headphones. Through God knew how many decibels of a military march?

She understood what he was thinking. A good solid wall of sound was the one thing in this place that kept her sane.

She indicated a pile of books on a table near the window. "I'm researching nineteenth-century composers for a book I'm working on and my door is always ajar."

She remembered it had been ajar — very fortunately — the night young Fleming had been walking in his sleep. She had just been in time to remove the headphones and rush out and catch him before he took a header down the stairs. He had awoken, white, sweating and speechless and she had marched him back to his bed with fiercely whispered admonitions never to do it again. As far as she knew he hadn't. She hadn't mentioned it to Roy Hammond and it was certainly much too late in the day to mention it to anyone now — least of all to the accusing figure sitting opposite her.

Fleming had seen David's dormitory on the first visit to the school. He asked to see it again. "Or are the boys about to go to bed?"

Brannigan said that the older ones were still at prep and that the younger ones would be at the first sitting for supper. He explained that the bed-time was staggered. "The young ones won't be up for a while. There's plenty of time to look around."

Normally the dormitory held ten beds. Fleming walked into the large austere room and counted only nine. David's bed and locker had been the second from the door. Both had been removed.

Brannigan noticed that he had noticed, but said nothing. The children in this room were the ten- to twelve-year-olds — old enough to understand and to be shocked and frightened. A tactful rearranging of the furniture had been done for their sakes.

Fleming's voice was quite controlled, only his eyes betrayed him. "Was there any other person in charge?"

Mollie Robbins, quite obviously dismissed by the words as less than useless, coloured but said nothing.

Brannigan answered, "The older boys have their own study bedrooms along the corridor — three are prefects. Mr. Hammond's own rooms are immediately at the bottom of the first flight of stairs. If there was a disturbance Mrs. Robbins would see it. In her absence the duty would fall to the senior prefect. The overall responsibility is Mr. Hammond's." He turned to Mollie and asked her the question that Fleming had decided was a waste of time to ask. "Apart from normal high spirits, was there any bullying — either of David or any other child?"

She gave him the answer that she believed he wanted. "Apart from the occasional pillow-fight — that sort of thing — no."

Brannigan said quietly, "Think a moment. And change your answer to yes if you have the slightest doubt."

As she looked back at him several pictures came into her mind. The Benchley child forced to lie on the bed while three of the other horrors forced toothpaste into his mouth. Young Kitson having his head held underwater in the bath until he almost turned blue. And Fleming — the child Fleming? As high-spirited as the rest at first — fighting like a demon when he had to — and then more recently becoming less noticeable. She couldn't put it to herself any other way. A fading of personality. A withdrawal. No longer a flaming nuisance. She felt a prickle of anxiety wondering what she had missed. In the general noise of battle one's ears weren't attuned to the whisper of pain.

Brannigan and the child's father were waiting for an answer. This time she gave it quite honestly. "I saw no-one hurt him."

Fleming gave a last glance around the dormitory. Shadows of leaves from a maple tree fingered the wall opposite the window like small curious hands. He saw the room as David had seen it and then abruptly he turned from it and went out into the corridor. The Robbins woman's uncertainty had come through to him like the crackle of static. She had seen no-one hurt him. She had seen bloody nothing. What was Brannigan thinking about in giving a woman like that a position of responsibility? The boys were a meal-ticket for her — nothing more.

The final authority, according to Brannigan, was Hammond. He asked to see him.

Brannigan explained that he was away for the day. It was possible that he had returned in the meantime, but he had no intention of looking in his flat to find out. He needed to speak to Hammond first and explain the deeper implications of the child's death. The circumstances were tragic before, but there had been no disturbing undertones.

Apart from the blindfold.

If the boy's jump had been suicidal he might have used the blindfold.

Or it could have been a game.

An accident.

As he walked down the stairs with Fleming he spoke his thoughts aloud. "I'm convinced David's death was accidental. Hammond is convinced of it, too. I understand that you want to speak to him and I can arrange for you to meet each other tomorrow. Some time in the afternoon. He has his school duties in the morning."

School duties that would include an interview with the solicitor, Tom Lessing, for a general briefing on what line to take.

Fleming said, "Three o'clock tomorrow afternoon at the entrance to the Maritime Museum. He will take me to the ship where David died and he will explain to me exactly what happened."

It wasn't a request mildly put, but a statement that brooked no argument. Brannigan, trying hard to mask his disquiet and failing, agreed.

"And now if you wish to interview any of the other

members of staff — or older boys — I'll take you over to the common room."

Fleming said, "No — the others can wait." Hammond, as he saw it, was the protagonist, the others would merely line up in a combined defence of the school. It would take more energy than he had at this stage — and more factual knowledge — to blast them apart. If any of them had contributed to David's death he would discover it in due time.

He had hoped to see Jenny again before leaving the premises, but knew it would do her no good to say so. Brannigan offered to drive him back to The Lantern and he accepted the offer. They drove in unbroken silence, the folder of David's work on Fleming's knee.

Roy Hammond returned to the school just before eleven o'clock and was making his way up to his flat when Sherborne, the science master, met him on the stairs. Sherborne told him that Brannigan wanted to see him, "But if you don't want to see Brannigan — consider the message not given. It seems the delectable Jenny gave Fleming a drawing by young David which indicates he was suffering the tortures of the damned." He tried to make it sound like a joke, his uneasy eyes embarrassed.

Hammond, who had spent part of the afternoon with his wife in an embittered argument during which she had flatly refused to return to him, stood still for a moment or two as if mentally bracing himself for this fresh blow. He didn't know what Sherborne was talking about. He would dearly like never to know. He should have walked out when Laura had walked out. He had been a fool to let her go with such a bland show of indifference.

Sherborne, expecting a response and not getting one, shuffled off down the stairs with a "Well, I've told you — if you want to know more before you see Brannigan, ask Jenny. One of your lads is with her in the infirmary now."

The infirmary, situated between Hammond's House and Sherborne's House, was reached by a corridor on the first floor. According to fire regulations there was a right of way when necessary, but the corridor was not normally used as a short cut between the Houses as Sherborne had used it now. Hammond wondered vaguely what he had been doing away from his own quarters.

As he approached the infirmary he could hear a child bawling and identified the sound as coming from Tim Sanders who could bawl louder than most. He was eight and seized upon any legitimate outlet for his grievance at being abandoned and incarcerated.

Jenny had her arms around him at the basin and was shushing him gently. "You've cracked a tooth, that's all. There's hardly any blood. Think what would have happened if it hadn't got jammed at the back of your jaw."

She looked over her shoulder as Hammond came in. "Did Mollie tell you?"

"Tell me what?"

"About young clever-boots here — the record-breaking, tooth-breaking, marble-sucker extraordinaire."

Sanders' sob squeaked upwards into a ragged gasping laugh. "What would have happened?"

"If it hadn't lodged where it had? You'd have swallowed the flipping thing — that's what would have happened."

"And been cut open to get it out?"

"Yes."

"And been sent home to get better?"

"Oh no, my lad, been sent right back here to the infirmary to me."

Sanders, breathing almost normally now, wiped his mouth with the back of his hand and then allowed Jenny to wipe both mouth and hand with a clean towel. She finished up gently mopping his eyes and was rewarded with the glimmer of a smile.

"Am I sick enough to stay in the infirmary now?"

"All right — just for tonight. Could you drink some warm milk?"

"Yuk!"

"Chocolate flavoured?"

He beamed, "Super."

Hammond said irritably, "You spoil them." He waited impatiently in the treatment room while Jenny took the child through to the small kitchen and let him help her make the drink. The infirmary dormitory held six beds and was adjacent to her own room. She settled him into bed and then returned to the treatment room and picked up the house-phone. Hammond listened to her side of the conversation as she spoke to Mollie Robbins.

"Six marbles in the child's mouth . . . A dare, I suppose. You know what they're like — they won't say . . . No, no damage — at least not much. He'll have to see a dentist . . . Yes, I know you have . . . Yes, I know you do. Anyway, I'll keep him tonight . . . A report? Well, yes — I have to . . . No — no harm done . . . No blame at all . . . Of course you can't." She glanced at Hammond. "He's back now. I thought you'd told him about Tim Sanders . . . Well, someone did. He's not psychic." She handed the phone to Hammond. "She wants to speak to you."

He made a negative gesture with his hand and then shrugged and took the phone. "It's all right, Mollie. Not a major disaster. Have the rest of the lads settled down again?"

He could hear her heavy agitated breathing. "Yes. There wasn't any sort of rumpus. I just happened to go in. He was gagging — his mouth wide open — I thought he had lock-jaw."

"Well, he hasn't. He's had some hot chocolate from Jenny and been put to bed. You can have him back in the morning."

42

He put the phone down before she could say any more. Her panic was out of proportion to what had happened. Normally she would have said something scathing about the awful child or the silly little brat. His own nerves, already taut, were on the point of snapping.

He explained that Sherborne had told him. "And he gave me a garbled story about David Fleming and a drawing. Brannigan wants to see me. Put me wise, Jenny. What's it all about?"

She found it difficult to explain. She was very much in the middle of a no-man's-land with a bias towards Fleming and sympathy for Hammond. The last few days had aged him. His thick fair hair fell untidily over his heavily lined forehead and he kept pushing it back with impatient nervous gestures as she told him about the drawing.

"Are you trying to tell me that the boy had a history of mental illness?"

"No, I'm not." She felt herself swing over wholly to Fleming's side. "The word is regression. I've never done any psychiatric nursing — but you know and I know that David was absolutely normal."

"So he just drew it for fun?"

"That's what I thought, but his father didn't. And when Brannigan saw it he didn't think so either. They saw it as a cry for help."

"To be rescued from the tortures of the damned."

She was startled. "What?"

"Sherborne's words — not mine."

She said quietly, "He could have had a shock. Brannigan asked me if he had. I said no. I think it's more likely he was bullied. And if I had to pick out anyone from your House who was likely to put the thumb-screws on him then I know who I'd pick."

"So you'd set up young Durrant as scapegoat, would you?" His anger was rising.

She answered with equal heat. "I'd set no-one up — and I'd say nothing unless I knew — but if I did know then I wouldn't protect him from his come-uppance. There are other kids still around — kids who need protection — those are the kids I'd think about."

"It's not like you to take an unfair dislike of any child."

"Child? At fifteen? When he looks at me his eyes undress me."

"Your job takes you amongst adolescent boys — he's not alone in that."

"Maybe. But none of the others makes my flesh creep." Her cheeks were hot with annoyance and she was breathing quickly.

He made a conscious effort to cool the argument. "I'm only asking you to be fair. Durrant, as far as you know — as far as I know — had that one fight with David. If you're going to start putting ideas about Durrant into Brannigan's head — or worse, into Fleming's head — they'll fasten their teeth into him like a fox's into a rabbit. If there's got to be a scapegoat — then at least I'm man-sized."

"I've no intention of putting ideas into anyone's head. I'm just telling you what I think. What I feel."

He went on quietly. "The boy is unprepossessing. His mother's a tart. His father dutifully acknowledges his existence — nothing more. Whatever stability he has we provide. Don't go kicking the floor from under him."

"But I've told you . . ." She gave up trying to justify herself. He was right to defend Durrant. She would have thought less of him if he hadn't.

After he had gone she looked in on Tim Sanders. He was sleeping peacefully. She remembered that it was the bed that had once held David. At twelve she hadn't tucked him in as she tucked this child in now, but she had felt the same affection for him as she had seen him sleeping. There was a little blood and saliva at the corner of Tim's mouth. She took a tissue from the bedside table and wiped it. What had he been trying to prove, she wondered? That his capacity for holding marbles in his mouth was greater than anyone else's? Or had someone forced them in against his will? Why didn't boys talk? Why did they perpetuate the myth of the honour of silence? Why didn't they split on each other? Why didn't they holler for adult help good and loud when they needed it? Why had David drawn a picture and thrust it at her? Why hadn't he screamed and cried and stormed and let the whole world know?

Obeying an impulse she couldn't resist she went back to the treatment room and found the telephone directory. It was almost half past eleven — there might not be anyone at the desk of The Lantern to receive the call — there might not be a telephone extension in Fleming's bedroom — there were a dozen good reasons not to make the call, but she set them all aside and made it.

He was sitting up in bed with David's book of essays when the phone rang.

The sound, like a bridge between two worlds, forced him back into the present time after wandering in another planet that had held his son. The essays, at times revealing, at times guarded, showed him a David he scarcely knew. A conformist David in a herd seeking the anonymity of what he believed to be the norm. Favourite author: Scott. Untrue. Any literary work older than the mid-century bored him to tears. Favourite holiday pastime: Climbing the Cairngorms. Untrue. On the one occasion he had taken him he had been so white-lipped with vertigo and fear that he had never taken him again. Why hadn't he mentioned pony-riding on the farm? He had loved the pony as much as he had loved his gerbil and he hadn't considered the latter too childish to mention. Did he really want to go in for scientific research — spelt resurch — when he grew up, or was that just a respectable idea grabbed out of the air?

When did the Navy start losing its appeal? Equally respectable. The airline pilot and the Naval officer — and now recently the scientist. The first two enthusiasms he had been in on and had bought him books with the appropriate backgrounds. In the normal way — if he had really meant it — the next holiday would have been spent with an embryo scientist. In what field? His own, perhaps. Electronics. A need to know — and the realisation that he would never know — frustrated him to the point of physical pain. He felt not only bereaved, but deprived. Others had walked with his son right up to the edge of oblivion. They had known his more recent thoughts. They had watched him, heard him, touched him. Several weeks of his life were to him, his father, clouded over, unguessable, never to be known.

Why in God's name had he blindfolded himself on that ship?

When they had gone climbing he had not dared look down at anything more than twenty feet. Had he worn the blindfold because otherwise he would never have summoned up the courage to jump? But wouldn't his way out have been a different way out. Wouldn't he have chosen some other way that would have frightened him less? And what was so terrible that it couldn't be faced? The term was halfway through — a few more weeks and they would have been together.

Impulsive suicide.

It happened to other children.

But David? Sane. Normal. Happy.

Happy?

When it happened he was alone — so Brannigan said. Brannigan could be wrong.

If not suicide — then murder?

The phone had been ringing for several minutes before he picked it up.

Jenny's voice. "I'm sorry, did I wake you?"

If it had to be anybody, then he was glad it was her. "No, I was awake."

She said awkwardly, "I just felt I had to say good night to you — and . . ."

He waited . . . "Yes?"

"I have time off tomorrow evening — from five onwards. I shall be at Nelson Street."

"Yes — well, I see . . . thanks." His mind was confused. He didn't know what he was saying. By the time he felt ready to speak to her she had put the phone down.

Four

THE NEXT MORNING a cold wind blew in from the sea carrying small flurries of rain. Fleming, who had slept little, killed the two hours between six and eight by walking along the coast road. The morning, sunless, lacked colour. The headland and the sea merged together in a blend of soft greys as if sketched in pencil. Only the wind, sharp with salt, was alive. The wind was believable, cold on his pores, uncomfortable, noisy and boisterous. It teased the sea so that it humped up into waves that broke hissing like snakes on the boulders below.

The Lantern served breakfast from eight onwards in a small dining room opposite the bar. True to its name, wrought iron lanterns flanked the fireplace and one of mullioned glass hung in the centre of the room. Fleming chose a table behind the door where he wouldn't be forced into conversation with any of the other residents. He had bought a local paper on his way in and read it with scant attention while his breakfast was being served. The world with all its problems mattered as little to him as a fly buzzing against a window pane. He didn't give a damn for any of it.

He missed the paragraph at the bottom of page three.

Mr. John Fleming, the father of the child who died tragically at the Maritime Museum, arrived at Marristone Port on Sunday. He informed our reporter that he would speak to him at a later stage when he was conversant with all the facts of the case. The autopsy is being carried out today and the inquest will take place on Friday. Mr. Fleming is staying at The Lantern after having spent one night only at Marristone Grange School.

Brannigan read the report aloud across the table to Alison while she poured him his second cup of coffee. The report was inocuous enough apart from the 'one night only' which was stiff with implication.

Her plump cheeks coloured with annoyance. "You brought him here and we did our best to make him welcome. He could have stayed here and had our support. He didn't have to go to The Lantern. He's impossibly belligerent. I think he's halfway out of his mind."

Brannigan said quietly, "Wouldn't you be, if it were your child?"

She conceded the point. "Possibly — yes — if we'd had a child. But I'd contain my feelings. I wouldn't go looking for the worst all the time. I wouldn't line up all the staff of the school and call in a firing squad because one boy played carelessly and fell."

"Or jumped — or was pushed."

"Utter rubbish! You can't believe that."

He was trying his best not to. If he hadn't seen the sketch he would have persuaded himself by now that it was an accident. He wished that Hammond could have seen the sketch. The description of it had far less impact than actually seeing it. Hammond had listened apparently without emotion. He seemed to have got himself pretty well in hand — or perhaps he was learning the knack of not letting his feelings show. He had agreed to see Fleming at the Maritime Museum with a curt, "All right — if that's what he wants!" but he had taken considerable persuasion to agree to see Lessing. His "You don't get counsel's advice unless you're accused — who the hell is accusing me?" Brannigan had countered with, "Nobody — yet. He's representing the school. I've already explained to you that the school must be represented. I've asked him to come up and have a chat with you here — informally."

Brannigan had contacted Lessing after leaving Fleming at The Lantern the previous evening. Lessing had agreed to come up to the school house at eleven.

There was one matter that Brannigan wanted to see to before Lessing arrived. It was quite likely that the request would be abortive, but he had to try. He waited until Alison had taken the breakfast things through to the kitchen and then he closed the door so that she wouldn't hear. He dialled Sam Preston's surgery.

Preston was facing the boy's father across the desk when the phone rang. It couldn't have been more inopportune, but at least Fleming couldn't have guessed the identity of the caller. He said brusquely that he would call back.

The sketch was on the desk between them.

The doctor repeated what he had begun to say when the phone rang. "I understand your anxiety. The pathologist will discover if there was sexual assault. He would discover that anyway, without any prompting from me, but I'll get in touch with him this morning if that's what you want."

"That's what I want. When will I know?"

"The report goes straight to the coroner, but in this instance as you're the child's father and next of kin you're entitled to be informed. You'll know later today."

He picked up the sketch again and examined it. If the boy had been assaulted then this sketch was dynamite. A prosecuting counsel using a psychiatrist's professional back-up could blow the school to hell.

He handed the sketch back. "You had professional advice from a psychiatrist at the time?"

"No. What's your medical opinion on it now?"

Preston thought: Lax of you, but lucky for Brannigan. "I'm a general practitioner — not a shrink. All I can do is to advise you to be open-minded about it until you know one way or another. Don't jump to conclusions. The boy might not have been touched."

"My God — if he has been!"

"Quite. But don't start thinking the worst."

He took out his prescription pad and wrote on it. "Take this to a chemist. They'll make the waiting period more bearable. And they'll help you to sleep."

Fleming returned the sketch to his wallet. He stood up slowly and took the prescription. He wouldn't use it, but it would be churlish to say so. Preston understood. Bloody pills, he thought. Bloody situation. But it was the best he could do. He saw Fleming to the door and then he put the call through to Brannigan.

"If you're about to ask me what I think you're about to ask me — then don't. The findings at the autopsy will be *sub judice*."

Brannigan guessed the situation. "Fleming was with you just now?"

"Yes."

"Obviously he showed you the sketch?"

Preston was silent.

"No comment?"

"I'm sorry."

"So am I — but I had to try."

"Strictly off the record," Preston said, "do you think the pathologist will find anything?"

Brannigan said heavily, "Strictly off the record — I don't know. If it happened then whoever it is isn't likely to go up on the roof-top and shout *mea culpa*. The sketch worries me as much as it worries Fleming — are we both exaggerating its importance?"

Sam, struggling between kindness and truth, did a bit of adroit side-stepping. "If the autopsy doesn't show anything then the verdict at the inquest should be favourable. There's no point in worrying in advance."

Tom Lessing, later that morning, said much the same thing. He was an old boy of the school and time had mellowed his memories of it. He had gleaned some carnal knowledge there and emerged heterosexual. He had been bullied to a point considerably short of dementia and done some bullying back. Muscles grown defensively — and offensively — large in adolescence had now shrunk back into flab. The school had given him the right qualifications to get into university and if he had had any sons of his own he would have unhesitatingly sent them there. That to him was recommendation enough. On the whole he thought that Brannigan was taking far too serious a view of the affair. It made sense to be legally represented — it made even better sense to keep everything in proportion. Hammond was sick to his gut already without Brannigan piling on the agony.

Lessing tried to keep the conversation light. "What it all boils down to is your contractual duty of care. If you failed in that duty — which I don't believe you did — action can be taken against you for breach of contract and for the tort of negligence. Tort. I tort I saw a pussy cat. Joke." He grinned and Hammond and Brannigan looked stonily back at him. He raised his thickly fleshed hand. "Okay — okay — I'll be serious — but if you'd waded the murky waters of the law courts as I have you wouldn't let this regrettable little affair worry you so much. Tort. Let me explain it. A tort is a civil wrong, not a criminal wrong. Let's say you took a bunch of boys on that ship and then left them to get on with whatever they were getting on with while you nipped off to the nearest pub for a drink. The child Fleming falls. Okay — you were negligent. You'd have cause to sit there sweating."

Hammond, unaware until then that he was sweating, surreptitiously wiped his hands on the plush arms of his chair.

"Did you nip off anywhere?"

"No."

"Right. Fine. I didn't for a moment think you did. How many boys did you take on the ship — eight — eighteen — twenty-eight — fifty?"

"Eight. I told you."

"So you did. A reasonable number. You kept the three youngest near you and told the rest to get the hell out of your hair — right?"

"I told them not to go to any other deck level without my permission."

"Young Fleming came and asked you for permission?"

"No. He went without telling me he was going."

Lessing leaned back in his chair and beamed. "But you, having second sight and the ability to look around corners, knew quite well he was going, so you told your three youngest to fall off the gangplank while you went and hauled him back?"

Hammond was silent.

"It doesn't stand up," Lessing said. "It just doesn't stand up. Would you call yourself a reasonable man, Hammond?"

"Yes — I suppose so."

"Do you think you'd pass the test of reasonable fore-sight?"

"What do you mean?"

"I mean the law might be an ass, but it isn't an un-mitigated ass. It protects you when all the circumstances are in your favour, and it slams you to the devil when they're not. In this case, I believe you did everything humanly possible to look after the boys in your care."

Brannigan asked, "What about the blindfold?"

"Well — hell — if one small boy wants to play Captain Hook and breaks his neck in the process — what's Ham-mond to do? Go and shoot himself? The boy crept off and played a game. He died. Tragic. I'm sorry. But you're asking me about Hammond and I'm telling you I think Hammond is all right. He discharged his duties to the best of his ability. If the boy had obeyed his orders he would be alive now."

Brannigan, who had explained about the sketch, men-tioned it again, but Lessing refused to speculate.

"That's outside my sphere. It looks to me like an ordinary, simple accident. If the coroner doesn't return a verdict of accidental death I shall be greatly surprised. Even if it were suicide, I don't see that anyone can get at Hammond with that. As I said before, he's not a mind-reader. If the child's jump were premeditated, how was Hammond to know? What you need, Brannigan, is a holiday. This accident has shattered your judgment. You need to get away for a bit and rest. The Grange isn't perfect — what school is? But it's a great deal better than most and when the British govern-ment starts putting back a little of the money where it rightfully belongs your numbers here will start to rise again. Marristone Grange had a damned good past and it will have an even better future once this little ripple in the pool is over and done with."

Brannigan glanced over at Hammond. If Lessing had

relaxed his tension then it was all to the good. He told Lessing about the meeting at the Maritime Museum with Fleming. "He requested it. I agreed on Roy's behalf. If you think Roy shouldn't go . . .?"

"Roy? Oh, Hammond." Lessing smiled weakly, but his eyes narrowed in thought. "Do you want to go . . . Roy?"

Hammond, intensely disliking the use of his christian name, said no, but he believed it would look bad if he didn't. "I have nothing to hide." It was like a cracked gramophone record, he thought, he kept on saying it.

"No, of course you haven't. But if you meet Fleming do you think you can make that clear? If you can't — then stay away."

"I think I can make that clear."

Lessing shrugged. "Go then. You don't have to. If I were you, I wouldn't. But I don't think you can damage your position by going. It all depends on how you handle it." He raised an interrogative eyebrow at Brannigan. "Are you going along, too?"

"I thought it might be advisable."

"Well, if you do, don't look so worried. No general ever won a battle by expecting to lose it."

"Battle?"

"Well — no — false analogy. No battle. No case. That's what I think. Animosity can breed its own sort of trouble, though. The ship is a particularly evocative rendezvous — a bit knife-twisting, I'd say, for all of you. Have a care."

Before leaving the school Lessing took a nostalgic walk on his own around the school grounds. Alex Peterson, Alison's father, had been headmaster in his time and Brannigan one of the housemasters. Peterson had run the place like a general who balanced strategy with force of arms. He had none of Brannigan's sensitivity. If this particular situation had been thrust upon him he would have refused point blank to contemplate placing the blame anywhere other than on the child himself. All that psychological mumbo-jumbo about a caterpillar on a bed he would have dismissed as balderdash. He would have been politely sympathetic with the boy's father, but he would have made it absolutely clear that the school had discharged its duty to his son. He would have been emphatic — unwavering — and as tough as the occasion demanded. Brannigan had a soft core. The ability to see the other person's point of view was useful in some situations, but not in this one. Brannigan needed to cultivate an inward eye. Alison knew all about self-interest. She took after her father.

The morning was becoming less chill and the clouds were lifting. He could hear the smack of a cricket ball at the nets and took the gravelled path through the yew trees down to the pitch. He hadn't been too bad a hand at cricket, though he couldn't remember liking it very much. Even the smell of the earth around here was evocative of his youth. The games master in his day had been a whippet-thin, small, fast-moving, ex-football pro called Patell — nicknamed Knees. The present sports master couldn't be more different. He was as hirsute as all the younger generation these days, thick, heavy, slightly pot-bellied, and with a lazy swing to his arm when he bowled. The ball got there though. The kid with the bat lunged out at it, missed, and the middle stump thwacked back into the grass. Innis, aware he was being observed, nodded over at Lessing and Lessing raised his hand in greeting and moved on.

Sports days in his time — in the fifties — had been well attended affairs at which boy met girl — other boys' sisters. Very decorous. Apart from one little broad he'd laid in a hollow in the long meadow. Even the long meadow in those days had been neatly mowed — apart from the rough grass beyond the wind-break of poplars. Now the grass was several inches high and even grew nettles. He ventured a little way into the wilderness in the general direction of the hollow.

He couldn't remember her face, or her name. He couldn't even remember the act, except that it had been his first with a girl — but not, he suspected, her first with a boy. She had smelt like wet grass with sun on it.

This was a good place, even now. Marristone Grange, like its meadow, had gone to seed a bit, but it was still a good place. If the grass weren't soaking his socks he would go to the hollow and linger there a little. It was a pity the day was so damp.

He stood for some while looking towards the wind-break and building up again a picture of what had happened beyond it before turning and retracing his steps up to the path.

Durrant, his hand over Corley's mouth, raised his head cautiously and watched him go. The child's teeth under his hand snapped suddenly at his fingers and drew blood. "You sodding little bastard!" Durrant's left hand took over from his right and pressed harder. The child, choking, tried to twist away. His stomach began heaving and green bile shot through Durrant's fingers. Sickened himself, Durrant drew back, and Corley, still vomiting, threw himself sideways and began running.

Lessing, startled, saw a child of about ten blundering out of the long grass and running blindly in his direction. The child's eyes were half closed and his skin was pallid. The sickness was around his mouth and on the front of his grey shirt. The school tie flapped around his right wrist and then fell off.

Lessing called, "Hey there — what's the matter?"

The boy swerved as if Lessing had delivered a hook to his jaw. Gasping he changed his direction and made for the cricket pitch.

Lessing picked up the tie and examined the slip knot. A noose. Intended for two wrists, apparently. The boy had pulled one hand clear. This time Lessing braved the wet grass, but when he reached the hollow no-one was there.

He stood and looked down at the flattened grass. There was vomit on a dock leaf and near it a tiny globule of blood. His mouth was suddenly sour with disillusionment. This had been his place — his place of youth. Now he would always see it this way. With disgust. With unease. What the hell had happened to the child — and how the hell had the other one got away so fast? He had no doubt at all that there had been another one. He made a quick search of the area and found nothing.

He fingered the tie, his mind on young Fleming. A child playing?

But this child now hadn't been playing.

Sick with fright. Just an expression before — but now it took on meaning.

Fleming senior had a case — or might have a case.

On balance it would be better if he didn't have a case. One rotten apple took some time to turn the rest bad. After the inquest Brannigan could be warned to start searching for that rotten apple — and damned fast.

In the meantime . . . He unknotted the tie and dropped it deep into the heart of a convenient bush.

Five

THE REVEREND SIMON SHULTER wore his dog collar on Sundays only, but on this morning made an exception. It looked incongruous with his blue sports jacket and jeans, but it stated his identity and cut out a lot of unnecessary explanations. He waylaid Fleming on his return to The Lantern after his visit to the doctor and suggested they should have a drink together. "I read the piece about your staying here in the paper this morning and I came straight over. The Marristone Grange boys attend my church. I knew David. We'd had a chat or two about confirmation."

Fleming's first reaction was a curt refusal, but he bit it back. Here was another stranger who had known his son. Confirmation? David? Religion hadn't played any role in his life at all. Ruth had arranged with her local pastor to have him christened, and he had a vague recollection of the ceremony in Ruth's non-conformist chapel. After that — nothing.

He agreed to the drink, one pint of bitter. Shulter ordered the same. They took their drinks over to the window recess where the watery sun gleamed intermittently and dazzled on Shulter's gold-framed spectacles so that he was forced to move his chair sideways to the table.

He was used to bereavements, but not to one of this nature and he made the usual speech of condolence hesitantly.

Fleming politely heard him out. Irreparable loss. It was odd how even a young cleric, just a few years out of theological college, fastened on to the well-worn clichés. This one had difficulty with his r's . . . not an impediment exactly, but one r too many which didn't quite come out as a burr. 'Deepest sympathy' would come next followed by 'God's will'.

Shulter said quietly, "I've made the usual noises at you. I haven't the gift of tongues, I'm afraid. There aren't any words for this. I have a young kid of my own. If it had happened to him, I'd feel as you feel. I think I can just about reach out and touch the edge of what you're feeling."

They sat in silence.

Fleming was the first to break it. "The autopsy is going on now."

"Try not to think of it."

"How can I help but think of it?"

"I know. But nothing is ever quite as bad as we imagine it is. I'm sorry I wasn't at the mortuary with you. Brannigan or Preston should have told me." He raised his glass of beer and watched the sunlight send little diamond flashes of foam into oblivion. That Fleming was seeing the autopsy in every small detail he had no doubt and he didn't know how to stop him seeing it. Now was the time to talk about the body and the spirit and he knew he didn't dare. This was raw and real. One word now delivered with unction rather than with belly-aching truth and the small thread of communication that they were beginning to establish would snap. Fleming would get up and go and he would chalk up another failure. It was his job to be here — God help him. Literally God help him. He didn't know how to help Fleming.

"Would you have agreed to the confirmation?" He asked the question for the sake of saying something. The answer no longer mattered.

"I don't know. I suppose so." It was a life-line of words and Fleming held on to it. Go on, he thought, talk to me. Tell me about the living David.

"Marristone Grange is C. of E. as you know. Confirmation is usual if the parents agree. I'd asked David about his own feelings on it and he said it was okay by him if it was okay by you. I sensed there was a close bond of affection between you."

"Yes."

"He didn't accept things easily. He questioned the Creed. Why would Christ descend into hell? He wanted chapter and verse quoted for everything. And then the Trinity — who or what was the Holy Ghost? He more or less accused me of inventing the Holy Ghost." Shulter smiled slightly. "He had a very literal mind, your son. Did you know that?"

"Tell me more."

"I take Scripture classes several times a term — not with any of the set examinations in mind, but just to get to know the boys. It's part of the Marristone Grange tradition. My predecessor had let it lapse and it seemed a pity. I remember asking David's class about their favourite Biblical character and David surprised me by saying Zaccheus. It had taken guts, David said, to climb that tree with the mob trying to elbow him out."

Fleming drew his beer towards him. He asked the question with some disquiet. "Did you sense that David himself was being elbowed out — by the other lads?"

Shulter's obvious surprise reassured him. "Far from it. He was likeable."

"He had no obvious enemies? No boy in his class that he was afraid of?"

Shulter, aware that the flat lands of pain had assumed the unpredictability of quicksand, began treading with caution. Enemies? What young boy didn't have enemies? An enemy of a day or a week metamorphosed into a friend of a day or a week. Marristone Grange wasn't terrorist country. Fleming was speaking of children.

"I can't imagine your lad being afraid of anyone. Certainly of no-one in my Scripture class. If something specific is worrying you, I think you should tell me more."

He listened, perturbed, as Fleming told him about the sketch. Consolation was called for and he tried to give it. "I think you're probably reading more into it than you should. He had been ill. Medication can have odd side-effects. He might have had a drug-induced nightmare and then drawn the picture."

"He might. It wasn't an explanation that Doctor Preston put forward. Perhaps he was trying to protect his pills as you are trying to protect the school." It was bitter.

It was also, Shulter thought, unjust. If he were trying to

protect anyone he was trying to protect Fleming himself. Whatever had happened it was over and finished. Fleming's acceptance of the boy's death was the first necessary step towards healing. The balm of Christian faith could only be applied when the wound was ready for it. The next question he had to ask would rub in salt, but it had to be asked.

"I'm not trying to protect the school. It just seemed to me that it could be physiological rather than psychological." He balked at the question and then eventually rushed it out. "I wanted to see you this morning to ask what you intend doing about the funeral?"

Fleming felt shock waves travel through his pores. His mind hadn't taken him that far. Shulter, aware how close he was to a breakdown, wished they were anywhere other than in a public bar. He moved his chair so that Fleming was partly screened from any curious onlooker.

Fleming, controlled again, felt the unexpressed sympathy. He imagined Shulter on the other side of a partition in a confessional. A quiet presence. Only the Church of England didn't have confessionals, did it? David hadn't been brought up C. of E. or R.C. His christening had been in the U.R.C. Which Godly trade union was to take charge of the burial ceremony?

Shulter pressed on gently with the practicalities. "I'll go with you to the undertaker. I wish I could take over all that side of it for you, but I'm afraid it's something you have to do yourself."

"I realise that."

"The funeral will probably be early next week — a few days after the inquest. Unless you decide to make other arrangements, I'll take the service — if you'll allow me to."

"I'm not a member of your church."

"That doesn't matter."

"Or even a believer."

"That doesn't matter either."

Shulter suddenly remembered some words of David's . . . not spoken to him but to another boy in his hearing after David thought he was out of earshot. "It seems to me you've got to flipping well take a heck of a lot on trust — do you think that's what he means by faith?" He debated whether or not to repeat the words to Fleming. They were so apt in this particular situation Fleming might believe he had made them up. He risked it.

Fleming heard David in the words. Trust. Faith. The words in the present context were hollow. David had trusted him and he in turn had trusted the school to take care of him. The kind of faith that consoled after the debacle was something outside his ken. He wished it were not. He wished he could go now with Shulter to his church and heave off this burden at the altar steps. He wished he could have a simple peasant faith — or the kind of faith that David was looking for.

He was aware that Shulter had something else to ask, and was wary of asking it. He waited and the question came with some hesitancy.

"The school has its own small chapel. At one time it was used for services. It's consecrated. Until the funeral would you like David's body to lie there — or do you want him to be taken to the undertaker's Chapel of Rest?"

Fleming's answer came with no hesitation whatsoever. "Anywhere but the school. The bloody place killed him."

Shulter, about to protest, thought better of it. Fleming's hatred was beyond reason. He hoped it was without just cause.

By three o'clock the day had begun to be beautiful. The morning clouds had shredded in the wind and though the rain was still sporadic it gleamed with sunshine. The inlet of water, channelled from the harbour, rolled in with a soft breathing movement that touched the old craft of the

Maritime Museum so that they, too, rolled and breathed and muttered like old men dreaming.

A Portuguese frigate painted in strong blues and crimsons splashed the water around it with paler blues and crimsons. Next to it the wind played in the lug sails of a Chinese lorcha. An elderly Thames barge and a Danish jagt moved in unison, their timbers creaking.

The paddle-steamers resisted the wind but responded to the water with slow rhythms evocative of ancient sea-shanties. The extraordinary peace of the place was suddenly shattered by the scream of a gull as it alighted on a tall thin funnel. From nearby a dozen gulls swooped in, calling and thrashing the water with their wings.

The small group at the entrance gate waited wordlessly and watched the gulls come and go. Hammond, standing a little away from the others, wished that he could have prevailed upon Brannigan to let him come alone. Brannigan at the last minute had decided to dilute the interview by bringing four of the senior boys, too. He had argued that Fleming would want to interview them anyway, and that the interview might as well take place on the ship where the accident had happened. Durrant, at fifteen, was the youngest and not sensitive. Masters, Welling and Stonley at sixteen plus were old enough to face the facts of the situation. In another year or two they would be out in the world. Fleming, no matter what his feelings were, wouldn't ride them hard. It was unspoken, but implied, that in their presence Fleming wouldn't ride Hammond too hard either.

Hammond guessed that Fleming would see it as a body-guard and add contempt to all his other emotions. He felt tired — even a little uncaring — as if the anxiety of the last few days had slowly exuded like pus from a boil. His mind refused to conjure up what had happened in detail, instead scraps of information he had dictated to the boys swam up to the surface like so much flotsam in the harbour. The

Sirius on her trip across the Atlantic had averaged 6.7 knots. The *Comet* averaged 6.7 in British coastal waters. Both better than the *Clermont*'s 4.7 knots. Shorter's propeller and Smith's screw of the early nineteenth century were the fore-runners of Ericsson's double propeller of the mid-nineteenth century.

Brannigan said, "He's just crossing the road by the traffic island."

Fleming saw the four boys before he noticed Brannigan and Hammond. Their stillness as they watched him approaching was almost hypnotic. He felt like an aircraft being beamed in on radar and then, breaking the pull of their eyes, he looked beyond them and saw Brannigan and another younger man who must be Hammond.

So this was the one. Tall — slightly stoop-shouldered — thick, fair hair badly cut — bony features — a long wide mouth — unrevealing eyes.

Brannigan made the introduction quickly and nervously, almost immediately turning from Hammond and drawing the boys forward. "These are the older lads who were on the ship at the time. I didn't think it was wise or necessary to have the younger ones along . . . This is Welling."

"How do you do, sir?" Welling dared to do what Hammond hadn't. He extended his hand.

Fleming took it. The boy lacked the usual awkwardness of adolescence. He had a glossy gracefulness. Masters was different in both physique and character. He was short and swarthy and mumbled inaudibly. His intense embarrass-ment struck a sympathetic chord in Fleming. This time he proffered his hand and the boy took it. Stonley, nondescript and silent, inclined his head stiffly and then moved quickly so that Durrant could come forward. Fleming remembered the name.

"Durrant."

"Yes, sir. How do you do, sir?"

There was a certain bravado in the tone, something in the expression in the eyes, that seemed to belong to another situation. He looked at a tall, rather ugly, gangling boy who had bashed David for voicing a preference for baseball. But not just that, he sensed something more. Durrant looked back at him and saw quite simply an enemy. The method of his extermination would become clear in time. His imagination was already feeding on it.

"You're the boy who objects to baseball, Durrant?"

The quick tongue touched the thick lower lip. "Only in this country, sir. He went on about it a bit."

"And you hit him — a bit?"

"Not hard, sir."

Fleming turned from him and looked at Hammond again. He indicated the boys. "Your idea?"

Brannigan spoke before Hammond could answer. "No — entirely mine."

"I fail to see the reason for it."

"You wanted an enquiry. The boys were there. They will be able to tell you what they saw or didn't see."

He had to agree to it. He wondered what kind of loyalty Hammond could drum up. The feeling of being behind enemy lines was strongly with him again. Hammond was being safely hedged around. The degree of his vulnerability depended on the boys and Brannigan himself.

Hammond said gruffly, "We can meet alone, if that's what you want, later on . . . I haven't tried to sympathise with you. Anything I say you'll probably misconstrue. If I say I'm sorry that David died — and I am, desperately and deeply sorry — you'll see it as an admission of guilt. I admit nothing. There was no negligence."

Fleming was silent.

Brannigan, deploring Hammond's attitude but not surprised by it, suggested that they should go into the Museum. He had already bought the tickets, including one for

Fleming. A party of Swedish students of both sexes went through the gate at the same time. They spoke loudly, cheerfully and incomprehensibly and looked with some curiosity at the group of boys and men who spoke not at all.

Their leader, who had some English, approached Brannigan. "Where is the position of the little ships, would you tell me please?"

Brannigan, cravenly glad of their presence but sufficiently strong-minded to make an effort to get rid of them answered curtly. "The models? In the shed — up those steps over there."

"The little boats of the primitive times, but not the models. The catamaran and the trees with the dug-out centre and the bamboo raft."

"They're in the adjoining shed — the shed next to that one. They are numbered in your catalogue."

"You are coming that way, too, please?"

"No. We are interested in the vessels on the water."

"And we also. Someone who would help with the interpretation we should be most happy to have."

Brannigan said firmly. "I'm sorry. It's not convenient for you to join us. You will find officials in each section. Ask one of them."

The Swede rejoined his group. He spoke to them quickly and bitterly.

Welling said in an aside to Masters, "How to make friends and influence people."

Brannigan overheard him. "In any other circumstances, Welling, your criticism would be justified."

"I'm sorry, sir. I understand the situation. I wasn't being critical."

"No? Amusing, perhaps?"

"No, sir. It was a stupid remark, sir. I'm sorry, sir."

There were times, Brannigan thought, when the honest-eyed, easy-tongued, commendably hard-working sixth-former got under his skin even more than Durrant did — which was saying a lot. Durrant had sparked up when Fleming had mentioned the baseball incident — rather like a bull being surprised by a matador's barb — but his expression had cooled down again to moroseness. Fleming's acquisition of that particular barb had surprised Brannigan, too, and disconcerted him more than a little.

The wind blew an empty sweet bag against Durrant's ankle. He picked it up, made a ball of it, and dropped it into the water. The waves took it and flipped it against the black painted hull of a yellow-sailed ketch.

Hammond spoke irritably, "There's a rubbish bin over there."

Durrant, not aware he was being addressed, didn't answer. His ability to switch off from reality into a more congenial and interesting environment had been acquired over the years. His growing physical strength and bizarre imagination combined forcefully into what he saw as a power-house in an alien city. He could people that city as and how he wished and dominate them — some in fact, others in fantasy. His mind was now on Fleming senior. Brannigan, as a heavy-booted Colditz commandant, was by comparison small fry. Around Fleming was an aura of blood. Pleasurably he felt a small crawl of fear. This enemy was in the world inside his head — and he was in the world outside it. He began smelling the water of the harbour again and saw that the sweet bag had rounded the bow and disappeared.

Brannigan went over to Fleming. "It would have been better to have come here after closing time with no-one around. I can still arrange to do that if you would like me to?"

Fleming saw it as procrastination. "Let's get on with it — now."

Hammond, surprisingly, brushed past Brannigan and took

the lead. He walked a few paces ahead of everyone, his head hunched between his shoulders, his arms swinging. The wind blew his hair into a parting across the back of his head so that his scalp showed white against the brown of his neck. When he stopped and turned, the wind took his hair the other way and he put his hand up in an irritable gesture and smoothed it.

"That's it. The *Mariana.*" He indicated a cargo vessel with a green and yellow funnel. It was pulling lazily at its anchor as if in a half-hearted attempt at freedom.

Fleming saw the name enclosed in a thin red-painted rectangle on the bow. *Mariana.* It was incongruously gentle. Like an execution chamber hung around with silk.

Now that he was here he wished he were anywhere but here. The thrusting reality of David's death had degrees of penetration. To bear the pain and yet retain his calm demanded of his strength more than he was capable of. His instinct now was to turn and go. He had seen and heard all he could take. He wanted no more of it.

Aware that his hands were shaking he put them behind his back and gripped his wrists hard.

Brannigan was beside him. There was sympathy in his voice. "There's no need to board her. Hammond can explain the positioning of the boys from here."

"We'll board her."

Hammond led the way down the gangplank. His voice assumed the slightly higher pitch he used in class. "Every time I take a group of boys on a ship we move around the ship as a group to discover the general lay-out of it. After that each boy, apart from the younger ones who stay with me, goes to work on the particular part of the project assigned to him. I suggest we move around the ship now as a group — afterwards the boys can take up their individual positions and you can question them individually, if that's what you want to do."

"That's what I want to do. But your guided tour can wait. I want to see the hold where it happened. Now."

What the hell was Hammond thinking, of, Fleming wondered. A slow build-up to a grand finale? Bridge deck. Boat deck. Lower deck. And now wait for it, Fleming, while the drums roll.

That he could quite easily kill Hammond occurred to him. He was emotionally capable of it.

Their eyes met.

Hammond shrugged. "All right. I wasn't trying to defer it. It was a duplication of the usual routine. I'm trying to present everything exactly as it happened." He turned to the boys. "Stay here. There's no point in your coming too."

The companion-way was short and steep. Fleming followed behind Brannigan and Hammond. The rail was wet under his hands, whether from the other men's sweat or his own he didn't know. The smell of the deck was of tar and carbolic.

Hammond explained, "There are three hatches. The one forrard is beamed. The tarpaulin was on this one as it is now. The other — where David fell — is just below the poop deck." He led the way.

His attitude was almost casual. "That's the one. There's no cover on it. There wasn't then and there isn't now. You might be able to screw damages out of the Maritime Museum for not covering it." He noticed Brannigan's expression and didn't care. The right words eluded him. A speech of sympathy at this point would be like offering milk to a cobra.

Fleming went over to the hatch and looked down into the darkness of the hold. It went down about fifteen feet.

David had stood here — or hereabouts — wearing a blindfold. The edge of the hatch would have come up to his thighs. An unwary step wouldn't have toppled him over. He had either climbed over or been pushed over.

The words that had been battering at the back of his mind for days came out as a whisper. "I don't understand." He repeated them to himself. *I don't understand.*

Brannigan, as grey-faced as he was, looked at him in silence.

Only Hammond appeared cool. "After the accident, I climbed down into the hold — down that iron ladder. It's not well lit, but I have a torch. Do you want to go down?"

Fleming turned to him. "Accident? Did you say accident? Look at the height of the hatch side. I only have your words his hands weren't tied."

"His hands were not tied. He could have rested them on the side of the hatch — perhaps have been doing handstands. Small boys don't have a sharp sense of danger — they're full of bravado. He could have been acting out some scene of daring from his imagination. He was imaginative."

"Was he? What else was he?" Very quiet — very level.

"I don't understand you."

"Was he sick? Disturbed? Unhappy? Frightened?"

"You're referring to the sketch?"

Brannigan said quickly, "I explained about it. I think, perhaps, its significance . . ."

Fleming interrupted him. He went on addressing Hammond. "I don't know what happened to my son — but I mean to know. Imaginative, you say. A circus act on the edge of the hold. Do you honestly believe that? Can you stand there now and look at me and say you believe that?"

Hammond made a helpless movement with his hands. "Anything I believe won't carry any weight with you at all. You're determined to think the worst. I'm sorry David died. I've said that before. If I say it a hundred times again it won't shift your prejudice against me."

"Too right it won't. His safety was your responsibility. Where the hell were you when you should have been right here?"

"I was looking after three small boys and trusting the rest to do as they were told."

"And David was told to do what?"

Hammond indicated the poop deck. "To get up there and make notes on the rudder machinery."

"That's asking a lot of a twelve-year-old."

"A twelve-year-old, an eight-year-old — they produce according to their ability."

"The sketch showed a regression to six. At what age level was the work you set him on the rudder machinery?"

Some of Hammond's aggression left him. "It wasn't done. He made no attempt to do it. I suppose you'll suggest now that he made a suicidal leap because I set him an impossible task."

"So you've dared use the word suicide at last. Be careful — you might become indiscreet."

Brannigan interrupted with some forcefulness. "We're not gaining anything by this. None of us knows what happened to David. We're here to try to reconstruct the scene — as far as we know it — and with the help of the other boys. Shall we get on with it? Or do you want to go down the hold?"

"I want to go down the hold." He added, "On my own."

Brannigan held Hammond's torch while he made the descent. Hammond went over to the rail and looked down at the water. The sun was edging the waves with silver. There was a sour sickness in his mouth and his chest felt tight as if Fleming had kicked him in the ribs; but still he was aware that the sun shone and the shadowed waters at the harbour edge were a deep cobalt.

He tried not to think of Fleming in the hold.

He tried not to think of Fleming's child.

The hold smelt of salt and seasoned timber and rope. The hatch above was a square of light. The light, like spilled water, flowed thinly and trickled off into a deep darkness.

71

Fleming bent down and touched the timbers almost directly under the hatch. His mind refused to see David lying dead. Complete identification with him wasn't possible. His own id protected him from what he couldn't take. He had reached the limit of his own separate existence and he couldn't over-step that limit. David had died. He himself was inexorably alive. As an act of contrition for his own limitation he wanted to lie on the timbers where David had lain, but he stopped himself. Brannigan was up there somewhere in the light. The private agony had to be contained in the mind.

When he climbed up the ladder again he surprised Brannigan by appearing so calm.

Brannigan helped him over the edge of the hatch. "Are you all right?"

"Yes."

"Then let's get back to the boys."

The boys, like abandoned guests at a macabre party, stood uneasily where they had been left. Brannigan felt a twinge of conscience that he had let them in for this. An interview up at the school would have been less traumatic. There, in their own environment, they had appeared adult enough and tough enough to be here — now he was less sure of them.

Hammond looked to him for a lead and when one wasn't forthcoming took command himself. "You all remember where you were on the day that David fell. We'll start with you, Stonley. The engine-room, wasn't it?"

"Yes, sir."

"Take Mr. Fleming there."

Brannigan said that he would go along, too. "You don't object?" This to Fleming.

"No. The boys are your responsibility." It came out heavy with innnuendo.

Brannigan's lips tightened and he said nothing. Stonley

skipped down the steps into the engine-room with some ease, but once there seemed to freeze into stillness.

Fleming with sudden compassion tried to get it over quickly. "How long were you down there?"

"I don't know. I didn't notice the time. I was making sketches."

"Did you see David at all?"

"Not since we arrived. We had our different jobs to do."

"Did you hear him call out?"

"No."

"Did you hear anyone call out?"

"No."

"When did you know that David had fallen?"

"I heard voices up on deck. I guessed something was wrong."

"Did you go anywhere near the hold yourself?"

"No." Stonley's hands were in his pockets. He took out his handkerchief and a half-smoked cigarette fell out. He put his foot over it.

Brannigan saw, but didn't comment. Stonley hadn't set the Maritime Museum ablaze — yet. One crisis at a time was sufficient. He looked enquiringly at Fleming. "Is there anything else you want to ask?"

Fleming thought — yes, but he doubted the wisdom of asking it. Stonley would probably freeze even further into the machinery and find no words to answer him. He tried the question: "If you had to describe David in a word or two — how would you describe him?"

"I don't understand you, sir."

"I know he was a few years younger than you, so you might not have had much contact. Can you be objective enough about him to say how he impressed you — or didn't you particularly notice him at all?"

"Oh, yes, I noticed him, sir." Stonley's foot drew the cigarette stub back towards him and he stood more comfortably. "He struck me as being . . ." he paused, looking for the word, "I don't know how to say it — one off from the herd, not a pack animal."

"You mean he ran alone — that the other lads disliked him?"

"No. They liked him. He played around with the other twelve-year-old kids — but sometimes he'd be alone and not seem to mind."

Fleming thought, you noticed him pretty intently — and was perturbed.

The other boys' answers to the same question were more superficial. Welling in the navigation house on the bridge said, "Happy and cheerful, sir," and added "absolutely" for good measure.

Masters, in the captain's cabin, blushed crimson with embarrassment and came out with a strangled "All right."

Neither boy had seen David fall.

Durrant, on the fo'c'sle deck had been the furthest away from the hold and he was the last of the boys interviewed.

He leaned back against the windlass as Fleming and Brannigan approached. Their footsteps were quiet on the deck but he magnified them in his imagination so that the thumping of his heart became the stamping of jackboots. A thrill of anticipation, almost orgasmic, prickled through his flesh.

He turned a suitably grave face towards Fleming and completely ignored Brannigan. "You want to ask me some questions, sir?"

Fleming on a sudden impulse tried a different approach. The situation — with this particular boy — was different. He said brusquely, "Tell me about it."

Durrant felt the impact of the challenge like a blow. His muscles tightened and then he slowly breathed out. "I wish I could tell you about it, sir, but I wasn't there so I don't know."

The waves were making soft little slapping sounds against the bow and there were far-off voices in the wind.

"Tell me what you were doing from the time you came here on your assignment until David fell."

Durrant looked past Fleming's head. The blue arch of the sky darkened in his mind and metamorphosed into a flat low ceiling of steel. The salt air became fetid and difficult to breathe. The winch behind him held the cold menace of torture. An exquisite pain flowed through his wrists where they touched the ropes.

"Are you all right?" Brannigan's voice.

He looked at the second inquisitor with ill-concealed disdain. "Oh yes, sir — just a little upset when I think about it, sir."

"You haven't answered me yet." No softness in this voice.

He reorientated himself. "My assignment was to make a sketch of the fo'c'sle deck and the windlass. I'm not good at drawing so I couldn't do it very fast. I hadn't done very much when I heard David shout."

This time it was Fleming who felt the physical impact of shock. None of the other boys had heard anything.

"The hold is at the stern — the other end of the freighter — how is it you could hear from here?"

"The wind carries sound, sir. If you listen now you can hear that party of Swedes talking on that freighter over there."

It was true. The other boys had been in enclosed areas.

"Go on. You heard him shout. What did he shout?"

"You don't shout anything when you're falling, sir. It was a muffled sort of scream." He looked to see if he had drawn blood and saw with satisfaction that he had.

Fleming, white-faced now, thrust on. "What did you do then?"

"Well, naturally, sir, I went to see. There was enough light

75

to see David lying down in the hold. His head looked wrong on his shoulders. He wasn't moving."

"And then?"

"Mr. Hammond arrived. He told me to stay where I was. He went down to look. When he came up again he went over to the rail. I thought he was going to be sick."

"Did he speak to you?"

"After going to the rail? He must have, sir, but I can't remember. When you've had a shock nothing you say makes much sense. I think he said something about fetching a doctor — or that might have been Mr. Sherborne."

"Mr. Sherborne?"

"One of the other housemasters. His boys were on the next ship — that one over there where the Swedes are now."

Fleming looked over at the other vessel. "So there were three of you standing near the hatch almost immediately afterwards?"

"No. Mr. Sherborne was amongst the people who began to come. It's like that with an accident, sir. There's nobody, and then there's a crowd. You don't notice them coming, but somehow they find out and they come."

"And then what happened?"

"Mr. Hammond didn't seem to know what to do so Mr. Sherborne took charge. He made Welling responsible for us as he's the most senior boy. He told Welling to take us into the cafeteria until one of the other masters could take us back to the school. We sat around a couple of tables and waited. We heard the siren of the ambulance — or it could have been the police. We couldn't see from where we were. One of the younger boys went over to the door to see if he could see anything and Welling belted him around the ear."

"When you looked down the hatch into the hold — before Hammond climbed down — could you see David's hands?"

"Yes, sir."

"Were they tied?"

"No."

"How was he lying?"

"On his stomach — his arms flung out on each side of him. Like this." Durrant went down on his stomach and demonstrated. He lay for less than a minute, but long enough to smell the tar of the deck and feel a rough splinter rub his jaw. He pressed his face into it and closed his eyes. The terror-dark engulfed him. He swam through it valiantly. The aperture of the escape hatch was closing razor sharp on his neck. He rolled over and his head touched Brannigan's fawn suede shoe.

He got up clumsily. "That's how he lay, sir."

"You're sure about his hands?"

"Absolutely sure."

"There's not much light in the hold. How clearly could you see?"

"Clearly enough to see that. He was a shape. Black against grey. His handkerchief was around his eyes. If someone is being executed then his hands are tied."

The knowing eyes looked at Fleming and measured with satisfaction the degree of pain that the image inflicted.

Brannigan expostulated, "For God's sake!"

Durrant turned to him. "Well, that's what his father thinks, sir."

Fleming asked quietly, "What do you think happened to him, Durrant?"

"I think he got bored, sir — so he began to play around. If you put a blindfold on you get muddled about heights and distances. He could have leaned over the hatch side and overbalanced." He smiled suddenly and his face became suffused with purity and simple gentleness. "I really do think that's how it happened, sir."

Fleming turned from him and began walking away.

Brannigan caught up with him. "Satisfied? His explanation was plausible."

Fleming glanced over his shoulder to make sure Durrant was out of earshot. "What's the matter with him?"

"What do you mean?"

Fleming wasn't sure what he meant, but he knew what he sensed. During some parts of the interview Durrant was a fairly typical fifteen-year-old boy — during other parts he wasn't there at all.

He wondered if Brannigan had a drugs problem at the school, but kept the thought to himself. Durrant certainly wasn't high — and the withdrawal was intermittent and for very short periods.

He tried to answer Brannigan. "He's not like the other lads."

Brannigan, knowing it to be true, refused to admit it. "No two lads are alike. Durrant hasn't a very stable background. It may reflect in his attitude."

"How does he behave towards the other boys?"

Brannigan answered with truth. "As far as I know, quite properly. No-one has ever complained."

Hammond was awaiting their return on the boat deck. He didn't ask anything about the boys' responses and it was Brannigan who volunteered the information. "The only one who heard anything was Durrant."

"Yes. As I told you at the time." Hammond took out a packet of cigarettes and lit one.

Brannigan mentioned Stonley's cigarette stub. "I didn't say anything. I leave it to you. He's probably having a quiet smoke down in the engine-room now."

"The least of our troubles."

"That's what I thought." Brannigan offered to round up the boys himself. "While you and Mr. Fleming have a talk — if that's what you both want to do?"

Hammond shrugged. "It's the object of the exercise. We

can winkle Masters out of the captain's cabin and have a talk there."

The cabin was full of polished mahogany and red plush. Everything was battened to the floor. Masters who had been fantasising about a voyage in the China seas took himself off with some reluctance and joined Brannigan and the other boys.

Hammond went and sat on the bunk and Fleming took the ornately carved Spanish mahogany chair near the flap-down table. Hammond's cigarette was Turkish and heavy. He shook his head as Hammond offered him one.

"So you and Durrant were the first on the scene?"

"Yes. We arrived within a few minutes of each other. It was a traumatic experience for the boy."

"I imagine he could take it better than most."

"If you were a schoolmaster, Mr. Fleming, you would be careful not to make snap judgments. You can't sum up a lad's character quite that fast."

"I take your point — but we're not here to discuss Durrant. How well did you know my son?"

"Obviously not well enough to read his mind."

Fleming thought, You smooth, uncaring bastard . . . He forced down his anger. "You spoke to him sometimes?"

"Naturally. I'm — I was — his housemaster."

"Earlier, you said he was imaginative. In what way?"

"Each House puts on its own Christmas entertainment. His contribution to ours was commendable. We didn't use all his ideas, but we used some."

Fleming had a vague recollection of David's mentioning a Christmas play. Jealousy that this man knew more about it than he did stung him, wasp-like, and he had consciously to brush it aside. "I've read his essays. There was one about being a research scientist. What field of research?"

Hammond was surprised. "Good God, I don't know! Is it relevant?"

"To killing himself? No. To knowing him — yes. You spoke to him. He was in your care."

"As you keep saying."

"And will keep on saying."

Hammond thought, What do you want of me, Fleming — my own blood, too? . . . He felt very tired.

Fleming didn't know what he wanted of Hammond . . . a weak, grovelling confession of negligence — or a flare-up into belligerence so that all the anger could spill over into an elemental tearing of flesh.

"Why should my son commit suicide?"

"No reason. I don't believe he did."

The silence was long and heavy. The ship creaked a little as it moved. Voices speaking in Swedish came softly from a distance and then, like the gradual turning up of a radio, were loud outside the door. It was flung open, letting in the fresh salt air and a dazzle of sunlight. The young bearded Swede felt the mood of the cabin much as a seaman becomes aware of the brooding atmosphere of an approaching storm. He mumbled an apology. "I disturb you. I'm sorry. I go."

Hammond got up from the bunk. "You've as much right to be here as we have." He addressed Fleming. "Have you anything else to say?"

"At this moment — no."

He, too, got up. The air out there where the Swede stood had a sweet fresh sanity. In here it was rank and bitter with proximity. He waited until Hammond had gone out through the door and walked a little way along the deck and then he followed him at a deliberate distance.

Brannigan, anxiously observing, saw them as the stalker and the prey. Both men were pale-faced, but showed no other outward sign of stress. Brannigan went to meet them. He spoke to Hammond first. "You've helped clear matters up a little?" Hammond looked through him and didn't answer. He approached Fleming. "I'm sorry the party of

Swedes disturbed you." The lie came out so palpably that he was sorry he had spoken.

Fleming's eyes rested on him contemplatively. "I am arranging to have legal representation at the inquest. A London solicitor — a friend of the family. She knew my wife and son."

"If you think it necessary . . ."

"I do. Who is representing the school?"

Brannigan gave the information reluctantly. "A local solicitor, with good background knowledge of the school and the circumstances."

"An old boy, perhaps?" It was a bullet fired at random and Fleming saw with surprise that it had struck its target. Brannigan, about to speak, was silenced.

"And the coroner . . . an old boy, too?" It was suave.

"No."

Fleming said, with deep sarcasm, "Pity — but you can't win them all."

Brannigan's resentment boiled over into anger. "Your implications are slanderous and totally unfair. For Christ's sake, we're not inhuman. What kind of reparation is there? What do you want us to do?"

The impossible, Fleming thought, give me David alive.

Six

JENNY SAW THE blue Fiat pulling up outside the flat, but paid scant attention to it. The street was used for parking, both by those who lived there and those who attended the local bingo hall on the corner.

She had spent two hours in the flat wondering if Fleming would turn up. His rather startled non-committal answer to her invitation the previous night had left her feeling raw and embarrassed. She had nearly opted to stay in the school, but had argued that it was her evening off and she was entitled to it.

Fleming wondered why she looked so disconcerted when she opened the door to him. She ushered him in with a rather fatuous, "So you've come."

"You asked me to."

"You could have refused."

"Why should I?" He went into the now familiar sitting room. He had seen this place — on and off during the day — as a refuge. Jenny as a person had withdrawn to some shadowy corner of his mind. Now once again she was flesh, human and humanising.

They stood and looked at each other. Her skirt was a dark maroon print with a frill around the ankles. A couple of inches of seam had come undone. He pointed to it. "You'll trip up with that."

"I'll sew it some time. The Fiat — it's yours?"

"Temporarily. It's on hire."

"It's as well you're fixed up. The Morris is in for its M.O.T. I came down by bus."

They sat opposite each other, cloaking a growing physical awareness with words. He told her about his visit to Preston in the morning and then Shulter's visit to him. "He was helpful. He drank with me in the bar of The Lantern while the autopsy was being carried out."

She edged carefully on to fragile ice. "Have you heard the result of the autopsy?"

"I phoned Preston before coming here. He was able to find out for me what I needed to know. There was no evidence of a homosexual assault." Repeating the words to

Jenny now he felt the same relief that he had felt when Preston had told him.

Jenny said, "That's one worry the less — perhaps the sketch meant nothing after all."

"Oh yes, it meant something — but I'm grateful it didn't mean that."

He told her about the rest of the day and his encounter with Hammond and the boys. "Is Durrant schizoid?"

The question didn't surprise her. "I don't know."

"I see you're not leaping to his defence."

No, she thought, there are plenty of others to do that, including Hammond and Brannigan himself. They built a protective wall of excuses around him. "Why do you think he's schizoid?"

He told her about the interview on the ship. "Schizoid might be the wrong word — you're in the nursing profession, put me wise to the right one."

"Bloody-minded?"

"Hardly that simple."

She didn't agree. Any community of any size was likely to include the right-minded, the high-minded, the simple-minded and the bloody-minded. Durrant was probably no worse than a dozen others only his personality happened to jar on her more. She didn't like one or two of the high-minded ones either. It was easy to label Durrant schizoid, but perhaps hardly fair. Certainly it wasn't a professional evaluation. She knew nothing about it.

"He's supposed to be the product of pretty awful parents. Marristone Grange is the balancing factor — a good environment."

"Is it?"

"Pretty average, I'd say . . . like everyone in it."

He smiled at her, but didn't come out with the obvious compliment.

She said, "If you want to eat — there's food."

83

"Later . . . Tell me about Hammond."

She wished he wouldn't place the onus of a personality analysis on her. "I don't know people any more than you know people. You saw Hammond today. You tell me about him."

He refused to have the question bounced back at him. "No — your version first. You've known him longer than I have."

She tried to be fair. "I don't know anything about his background, but he strikes me as the type who went to a school like Marristone Grange himself. He slipped into the mould quite easily. His wife didn't. That's why they split. He put the school before her. He's regretting it now, I think. At this moment I see him as lonely. He's made one or two passes at me — unsuccessfully."

"Then he's normal?"

She looked for an undertone of humour and didn't find it. "Oh, I see. Heterosexual as opposed to the other. Well — yes. Well — emphatically yes. In any case, that doesn't arise any more, does it? David wasn't molested."

"No. But the sketch still hasn't been explained. Durrant perturbs me. Hammond's indifference gets·so much under my skin I could . . ." He caught her expression and stopped.

"He's not indifferent. He's shocked and worried. I don't expect you were easy with him — how could you be? He probably met you with all his defences up. Everyone wants to survive, Roy Hammond included."

"He'll survive." It was bitter.

"Yes — why shouldn't he? David died — and even you will survive that. You have to, it's the way of nature." She sensed that her defence of Hammond had angered him, but didn't care. Today he was more normal than he was yesterday. The rage in him had to burn itself out some time. He looked better physically. The cold, white look of grief was less evident. Yesterday she had literally nursed him through a crisis and then crashed him back into it again by producing the sketch.

"If the sketch were mine," she said, "I'd tear it up. It's a sick thing. It's not David as he was. It isn't even proof of anything. He wasn't sexually assaulted. You can't use it at the inquest. Get rid of it — as you got rid of all the others. That's what he'd want."

He was silent for two or three minutes. How the hell did she know what David wanted? Who the hell was she trying to protect?

She sensed his withdrawal and then slowly was aware that he questioned his own reaction and was trying to reach out to her again.

He said brusquely, "It's the last thing I have belonging to him."

"But not the last thing he'd want you to have. You have his essays — his books."

"It's a cry for help."

"Is that how you want to remember him? Crying for help? He laughed, too, you know. For most of the time things were good for him."

"For most of the time. And the rest of the time —? By Christ, you're not asking me to ignore the rest of the time — the last few days? I've got to find out why."

"Agonising over that sketch won't make the finding out any easier. You may never find out. What are you going to do — carry that sketch around for the rest of your life saying, My twelve-year-old son drew this —?"

Anger burst in him like a deep subterranean explosion. "Who are you doing this for — Hammond — Brannigan? Which of them set you up?"

Her astonishment was obvious and then her anger rose as bitterly as his. "I'm not asking you on anyone's behalf. Keep the bloody thing. Sleep with it under your pillow. Go quietly mad over it. Set David up in some sort of lunatic shrine. I knew him as he was. I remember him as an ordinary nice kid. If I were his mother I'd say — okay, I've heard you, I'll do what I can. Point made — and now let's get rid of it." Her voice shook. "But then, don't take any notice of me. I'm not his mother. I'm the school matron who entices you here to persuade you to tear up your puny bit of evidence. Evidence of what — for God's sake? Look, Your Honour — Mr. Coroner or whatever you're called — this is proof beyond any doubt that David killed himself."

She paused to draw breath.

His own anger was spent. He didn't know how to heal her hurt. He could feel her pain in his own throat as she struggled with the words. "I was protecting you."

"I know. I'm sorry."

"Keep your sorrow. I'm tired of it." She was lashing out, saying anything, not meaning it.

"That I understand."

"Do you? Can you look outside yourself long enough to understand anything? We're the enemy, don't forget."

"Not you."

"Oh yes — a few minutes ago you'd lumped me with the rest of them. Hammond. Brannigan. The school. David's killers. What do you think we are — a mob of murderers?"

"Someone . . ."

"Oh yes, someone — perhaps. And then again — perhaps not. Don't you want to believe in an accident? It could have been, you know. He could have been careless, kids are — they fall. What's wrong with that explanation? Not dramatic enough? Someone has to pay — is that it? What sort of cash value do you put on David?"

She got up before he could answer and left the room. The hot tears of rage and hurt were spilling over and running into the corners of her mouth. Shame was no small part of her emotions, it had been an appalling thing to say. She went into the bedroom and sprawled face-down on the bed pressing her face into the pillow.

She didn't hear him following her. The way she was lying reminded him of David in the hold of the ship and he put his hand on her shoulder to break the image. And then the image was gone and he saw and felt only her. Until now he had believed his sexual drive dead or anaesthetised. The explosion of anger had been like the bursting apart of a carapace. The protective conventions had gone. He had come to apologise anew, to try to make up for the hurt he had caused her. But now that was forgotten.

His hands tightened on her shoulders and he drew her to him.

She tried to push him from her. "I'm not a bloody whore!"

And then she stopped struggling — wanting it, too. Neither hatred nor love had any part of this.

There was no gentleness in their lovemaking, but there was gentleness afterwards as they lay together. He touched her breasts and then took his hands down in long caressing movements over her thighs.

She answered him, "Yes," meaning "Again."

She had slept with others before, but it had meant nothing. This time, in an aura of rage and pain, her initiation into a full awakening had been superb.

The second time, he took her slowly and tenderly and then leaned up on his elbow and looked down at her. With Ruth, and all the women before and after Ruth, the sexual preliminaries had been civilised. He had never forced himself on anyone before. He wondered if he would have drawn back if her resistance had lasted more than a moment or two. He should, he knew, be dismayed — not euphoric — and tried to frame some sort of an apology.

She put her fingers across his lips. "Don't."

"When I followed you in here I never intended . . ."

"I know."

He lay down beside her again and held her to him. Physically he felt eased and pleasurably tired. David, truly dead, had passed into temporary oblivion. They lay for a long while in total contentment.

He didn't think about David again until he drove her back to the school later that evening. It had been a wholly satisfying and healing limbo of forgetfulness and he emerged from it reluctantly and with an irrational sense of betrayal. That he could forget David in an act of love with a girl he hardly knew showed a facet of his nature he hadn't been aware of. He backtracked in his mind everything that had led up to it and remembered the sketch.

"I'd like to give it to you — and let you tear it up. A present of peace to David. But I can't. It may be worthless evidence — or it may not. I can't risk destroying it. Not even for you."

She accepted that his mood was in a downward swing again. The sketch had triggered an emotional reaction that had kicked down barriers — what he did with it now was up to him. She deplored its existence, but she was grateful for it, too.

She said with surprise, "I've never before slept with a man and not known his christian name."

After being briefly startled, he felt the sudden sanity of humour bubbling up into surprised laughter.

"John."

She said dryly, "Well — thanks for the introduction."

He told her he would be going up to London to contact his solicitor the following day. "I'll be back tomorrow night, but probably too late to get in touch with you. I'll see you the day after tomorrow."

"I'll be on duty at the school."

"Whenever you're free." He went and opened the car door for her. "That is if you wish . . . if tonight . . ." He fumbled clumsily with the words, not sure how to put it to her.

She said calmly, "Tonight was . . . unexpected . . . and . . ."

"And?"

"Good and natural and I'm glad it happened. You've just dropped me off at Marristone Grange, not at a nunnery." She reached up and kissed him. "Maybe, I even love you a little."

She walked swiftly up the drive before he could answer.

Entering London, after the days in Marristone, was like entering an orchestra pit with an atonal orchestra in full swing. The noise assailed Fleming as he drove and the traffic forced his concentration.

Thirza, in partnership with two others, had an office off Regent Street. It was a semi-basement and uninviting on the outside. Inside, it spelt money. Thirza's own room off the small reception area was furnished with antiques. Her desk, he remembered her telling Ruth with some pride, had cost just under a thousand pounds. She had always tended to talk money — which was surprising as she had never lacked it. Crayshaw, Bradley and Corsham had been a family firm for nearly half a century. Her father, Reginald Crayshaw, had made her a junior partner immediately after she got her law degree. Now, fifteen years later at thirty-eight, she had inherited his share and took a third of the profits, which were considerable.

When Fleming was shown in she was reading a copy of the account of David's death which her secretary had typed for her after phoning the *Marristone Herald* that morning. She hastily slipped it into a drawer and rose to greet him. "I was most awfully shocked. I didn't know until you phoned. It might have been in the dailies — I didn't see."

Her embarrassment and her concern paradoxically made the meeting easier than he had expected. Here was a case of meeting someone halfway — of making things easier for someone else. She had never been a demonstrative woman. Her two husbands had come and gone without leaving an emotional ripple and she had reverted to her maiden name. Ruth's assessment of her: introspective, work-orientated, but a kind and true friend, was probably based on the fact that Thirza kept her marital problems to herself and never poached on Ruth's territory. Any other woman at this sort of meeting would have given him if not a quick sympathetic peck on the cheek then a warm sympathetic squeeze of the hand.

He took the chair she indicated and said easily, "It's good to see you again. It's been a long time."

"Twelve months — no, more than that, nearly two years."

She had done something to her hair, he noticed, or else she was going prematurely grey. It looked attractive with her dark eyes and warmly tanned skin. Her olive green silk dress was finely pleated from neck to hem and fastened at the throat with six small buttons. He contrasted her with Jenny. Sartorially and in every way they were poles apart.

Aware of his scrutiny and a little puzzled and a little flattered by it she waited for the boat to be pushed out into the water. He looked ill, but that was to be expected. He appeared to be extremely controlled, but she knew him well enough from the old days not to be taken in by it. He had adored the child.

She said, "Yes, well — whisky, coffee? Or nothing now — an early lunch? I've booked a table."

"Thirza — the wound has been taped over. I'm not going to embarrass you with a show of blood."

"No — but I understand what you feel. I'm not good at saying so."

"Take it as said."

"Lunch, then — in half an hour? At twelve?"

90

"Don't be afraid to speak to me. David is dead. I can say it."

"Yes." She was silent. Her fingers caressed a crystal paperweight and a shaft of sunlight threw a reflection from it on to her jaw where it hovered like liquid silver. She moved her chair back and opened the desk drawer. "I managed to get this." She took out the typed paragraph. "I guessed the local paper would cover it."

He read it. "Would you understand me if I told you that I would like to see the school razed brick by brick?"

So the boat was being pushed out and the waters were stormy.

"You hold the school responsible?"

"Of course. I sent him there in good faith. They killed him." All vestiges of Jenny's defence of the school had cleared from his mind. If his hatred of the school were paranoid then he accepted the fact of his paranoia. He, on David's behalf, stood in the arena.

Thirza had been trained not to let her astonishment show. "You mean — you don't think it was an accident?"

He told her about the blindfold. And then he took the sketch out of his pocket, and put it on the desk. She noticed that as he explained about that, too, he kept his eyes carefully averted from it as if it were an obscene thing that sickened him. "I want you to keep it and use it at the inquest — if it can be used — to show David's state of mind."

She doubted if it could be used. Without professional psychiatric backing it carried little weight. "Death due to failure of contractual care might bring you damages. I can't do any forecasting on that without the full facts."

Jenny's words about setting a price on David come back to him. "Damn it, I don't want damages. If any money comes my way, then it goes directly to charity." He tried to explain. "If the school, or someone in it, can be proved responsible for killing David, then I have every intention

91

of taking an eye for an eye. One child dying is one child too many. Especially when that child is mine. The school lives on its reputation. If it can be proved to have stepped out of line, in any way whatsoever, then I shall see to it that it won't live long."

."You're capable of a lot of hate, John." She added before he could answer, "Inversely proportional, I suppose, to your love of David. It's a pity this happened in so short a time after Ruth."

"You think my reaction is abnormal?"

"No — under the circumstances, perfectly normal."

"Then you'll represent me at the inquest?"

"Of course — but in my own way. You'll have to leave it to my judgment. I'll use the sketch if it seems relevant. Have you any idea what an inquest is? It's simply an enquiry held in a coroner's court. Afterwards it may go further. The extent of your pain won't bend or influence the course of the law. You can't be clear-minded, but everyone else will be — including me." She put the sketch in a manilla envelope and put it in the top right-hand drawer. "Now tell me about it again. All of it. Every small detail. I'm switching on a tape-recorder, but don't let that inhibit you. Just pretend it isn't there."

After some preliminary awkwardness and hesitancy he began his account. For most of the time she didn't look at him and only occasionally prompted him. When he had ended it she knew that he had invited her to fight a lost cause.

It was politic not to say so.

"Well?"

"Hammond could have treated you with more courtesy."

"Is that all you have to say?"

"I could sing a duet of hate with you — and I will if it will make you feel better. But legally — well, I don't know. I'll give you all the back-up I can."

If she couldn't show more enthusiasm for the case, he

thought, then she might as well unfurl her banner on the other side. That she would do her best he had no doubt. She was basically honest and highly qualified. No-one else, he supposed, would show any enthusiasm either. The emotional involvement was his. He couldn't expect anyone else to share it.

She took him to a small Austrian restaurant. The whole set-up was very elegant and extremely expensive. Jenny's tablecloth, like her skirt, had a loose hem. Her kitchen was shabby and comfortable and the sun shone in it.

Thirza, disconcertingly, cut across his thoughts. "These days — have you anyone?"

He hedged. "I'm not living with anyone."

"Neither am I. Where permanent relationships are concerned, I'm disaster-prone. I find the single state extremely peaceful." She held her wineglass up to the light. "Have you noticed the sediment in this? Should we send it back, do you think?"

"Are you changing the subject — or do you seriously want me to send it back?"

She put the glass down and smiled. "It's hardly worth the bother. I'm changing the subject. You seemed embarrassed when I asked you that question just now. Will you be staying in London tonight?"

"No, I hadn't planned to. I shall be using this afternoon to call in at the main office. I walked out of the Bombay office with no notice whatsoever. They'll cope, of course, but they'll need to be informed of what's going on and when I'm likely to be going back."

"And when will that be?"

"The funeral will be some time next week."

"If my being with you at the funeral will help . . .?"

"It's kind of you." It was neither an acceptance nor a rejection.

"How did you cope on David's holidays?"

"He travelled with me most of the time. And I've kept a small flat here in London. Most of his clothes and belongings are there. They'll need to be packed."

She suggested that they might meet early that evening in his flat and pack them away together. After the funeral, she knew, would be soon enough, but if she were to help him at the inquest then a deeper knowledge of him and events was necessary and this was one way of gaining that knowledge. They would have an hour or so together. Seeing David's possessions would loosen him up emotionally. If she were to get anywhere she needed a gut response. It wasn't just a case of representing him at the inquest, it was a case of finding out how best to ease him through it.

He arrived at the flat in Marylebone half an hour before her. It was on the second floor of a Victorian house and David's first reaction to it hadn't been enthusiastic. He had been used to a garden and a green outlook. Once he had a permanent base, he had told David, he would get a house for the two of them again. In the meantime this had to do. David had asked how long was temporary and he had answered a year or two. A year or two, David had said, was survivable. He could put up with most things — even this — for a year or two.

The memory of the conversation was surprisingly clear. Since Ruth's death David had done a great deal of putting-up. The flat. The school. And always the promise of a future that never happened. It was bitterly ironical that a permanent appointment to the Paris office had been offered him that afternoon. He had surprised Thomson by asking for time to think about it. Yes, he told Thomson, he knew he had put in several applications for a non-travelling job — and yes, he liked Paris. But he wanted time to think. Thomson had given him a week. He hadn't added "Until after the funeral," but it had been implicit in his tone of voice. "By then," the look in his eyes had said, "you'll be rational enough to pluck the plum that's offered you." The job carried a substantial rise in salary. Had it been offered him as short a time as a few months ago he and David would have been settled into a comfortable environment by now and David would have been attending a local lycée.

He would have been alive.

The flat had a stale empty smell and was veneered over with dust. He went into all the rooms and opened the windows. David's bedroom was festooned with model aeroplanes. Three balsa-wood Spitfires suspended from the ceiling with white thread caught the breeze from the open window and became entangled. A fragile, red-painted propeller tore off the framework and spiralled to the floor. He bent and picked it up. They had spent a wet Sunday making this one. David had had glue on his hands and had struck a match to melt some sealing wax. The glue had ignited and the palm of his hand had been burnt. It had taken a couple of weeks to heal. During the couple of weeks the finer, more precise areas of model-making had been taken over by him under David's direction. The Messerschmitt on the chest-of-drawers had been almost entirely his own work. David had got bored in the middle of it and had gone off to read a book. "Not bad for a beginner," had been his comment when he saw it finished. His suppressed grin had sparked up in his eyes as if laughter were light suddenly blazing.

He wished that Thirza wasn't coming. This was a private place. His and David's.

But when she came he accepted her intrusion and buttressed himself behind a polite seemingly casual façade. He took the large pigskin suitcase from her and put it on David's bed. "It's his winter clothes, in the chest-of-drawers and wardrobe. The rest of his stuff is at the school." He couldn't bear to watch her and told her he was going to buy an evening paper. "I'll be back soon."

He gave her an hour.

When he returned, the suitcase was standing in the hallway, locked and strapped. He repressed an urge to touch it. She called out to him from the sitting room. "I've a couple of drinks poured. Bourbon. You don't seem to have anything else."

He thought of Jenny's whisky.

He wished Jenny had packed the suitcase. Hers wouldn't look like this. It would be battered and bulging and everything in it would have been put away with love.

"Thanks. I'll be with you in a minute." He went into the bedroom and saw with irrational relief that the aeroplanes were still there. She followed him. "You'll need a large cardboard box for those. I didn't think of bringing one."

"I'll see to it."

She moved past him, slim and elegant in the white trouser suit she had changed into, and opened a bedside cupboard. "There's a microscope here. It looks a good one. Would you like me to sell it for you?"

"For Christ's sake!"

She couldn't understand why that should penetrate his armour when nothing else seemed to. It was a pity he had gone out while she had done the packing. She had imagined him sitting on the bed talking to her while she had done it.

She said equably, "The clothes will go to a children's charity. They could use the money from the microscope, too, if you agree."

He agreed. He wished she would stop talking about it.

"And there's a stamp collection. I don't know if that's valuable or not?"

"Not."

"The microscope — what was he going in for? Your line?"

"Scientific research — spelt with a u." And nobody knew what line.

He suggested they should have the drink. Dinner hadn't been planned, but under the circumstances it would be churlish not to invite her. She had been kind. She was representing him at the inquest. She was a friend of long-standing.

The thought flashed into his mind that he had known Jenny for two days.

Time was a clown that stood on its head and made rude gestures. He was offered the Paris posting — now. David had lived twelve years. Jenny's warm familiar flesh had been warm and familiar for a few hours only.

He needed her.

In the middle of his shock and grief he needed her.

He should have no thought for anyone but David, but he walked a behavioural maze and struggled through to her at the centre of it. If anyone could lead him out into sanity again, then she would lead him out.

Thirza said, "I found this in David's anorak pocket." She handed him a snap, dog-eared at the edges. It was of Ruth standing in a winter garden with snow on her boots. Boris, the red-setter puppy they were looking after for a neighbour, was pawing at her fawn mackintosh and leaving wet marks on it. On the back David had written in blue crayon, *Mum cross with Boris.*

It wasn't a particularly attractive snap of Ruth, but it had caught the moment. Remembered laughter. David had been using up the last two snaps on the reel. The other one had been of him and Ruth together after Boris had been banished to the house. David had focussed it badly and it had come out blurred.

Thirza commented, "Not a good one of Ruth."

"A happy one."

"She's scowling at the dog."

"Afterwards she laughed."

"Talk about her to me, John. And about David, too. I

97

need to know to understand. You've given me facts — as you see them. If you believe that David was unhappy, I've got to know more about him — about you — about his reaction to losing Ruth. I think you may be making the school a scapegoat. I've got to know more."

He looked at her helplessly. "He was recovering. Up to this last term — he was recovering. Then something happened. He drew that bloody sketch to show that it was happening."

"And gave it to the school matron." It was dry.

"Who cared about him."

"As a mother substitute?"

Surely she was too young — even in David's eyes? "I don't know."

"But you might know by talking about it."

"I can't." It came out flatly. Ruth. David. Jenny. They were like three portraits in his mind. A private room housed them and Thirza had no entry to that room. She would have to represent him at the inquest as best she could. He put the snap in his pocket. "If the time is too short for you — or if you don't honestly feel you want to go on with it . . ."

She interrupted him. "I want to help you. If the school is to blame, we'll know soon enough and I'll take it further. But if the school isn't to blame — then you must accept that, too. Whichever way it goes, stop blaming yourself. No father could have done more."

She refused the invitation to dine, saying she preferred something casual and easy at the pub on the corner. The conversation had been casual and easy, too, and she had failed to break through to anything deeper. Understanding her motives he had drunk lightly, making the drive back an excuse for not over-indulging. She was not enemy-territory, far from it, but he didn't want her kindly probing either. She had the facts, but if she were hoping for an emotional outburst then she could sit here until closing time and not get it. Jenny had seen his agony and his rage — and felt the brunt of both. He couldn't let go with anyone else.

It was Thirza's suggestion that she should spend the following night at Marristone Port. "Even though the inquest isn't until the afternoon, I don't feel like risking heavy traffic on Friday morning and being delayed."

He agreed. "But The Lantern is hardly your style. The Strand on the west side of the Port looks more comfortable."

In a shy, awkward gesture she touched the back of his hand with her index finger. "If it's not too squalid for you, I'm sure I'll find it perfectly acceptable. Book me at The Strand if The Lantern's full, but try The Lantern first."

He promised he would and that they would have dinner together at The Lantern either way. He hoped he had put some enthusiasm into the invitation. She was an extremely attractive, kindly woman. If Ruth had been master-minding his present campaign she would have spirit-smiled her approval. He wondered, fleetingly, what she would have thought of Jenny.

It was ten o'clock when he took his leave of her at her flat in Knightsbridge. The June night was prematurely dark and a light rain fell. By the time he reached the outskirts of Marristone Port the rain had become intermittent and the moon shone on the dark country roads. He didn't notice the child, Corley, pressed up against the wall as the car passed. Corley had pulled his school cap across his face and buried his hands in his mack pocket so that no white skin showed. It wasn't until Corley was well clear of Marristone that he ditched his cap and began looking out for a lorry going in the opposite direction. To hitch a lift in a private car would probably result in his being returned to the school or murdered. He regarded both with equal horror. But to climb on to the back of a lorry travelling more or less in the

99

general direction of Somerset — without the lorry driver knowing he had climbed on to it — shouldn't be particularly hazardous. Provided he could find a parked lorry — or a lorry toiling slowly up a hill. He trudged on in the darkness discovering as the night wore on that parked lorries and slow lorries weren't exactly thick on the ground. And the only one he could have boarded was going the wrong way.

Seven

CORLEY'S ABSENCE, AS Corley himself had anticipated, wasn't discovered until breakfast-time. Travers, one of Sherborne's senior prefects, brought the news to Sherborne. Sherborne, after a quick search of the premises went over to the school house and informed Brannigan.

Brannigan, still breakfasting with Alison, exploded, "Christ, that's all I need!" He had spent a restless night trying to reassure an insomniac Alison that all would go well at the inquest on Friday.

At Sherborne's news her face took on a yellow pallor and she sat silently looking at him, her breakfast plate pushed to one side. Brannigan tried to control his own reaction. He said to her abruptly, "He can't be far." And to Sherborne, "I'll walk back to school with you." In passing Alison he dropped his hand on her shoulder and squeezed it gently. "Just a prank, probably. Stop worrying."

On the way over to the main building Sherborne gave him all the details as he knew them. "My wife and I went to bed shortly after eleven. She had made the dormitory check at ten — it didn't seem necessary to do it again. All the lads were in bed then."

Brannigan said sharply. "Or perhaps seemed to be — you know the old trick with the pillow."

"Well — damn — she didn't go round prodding the lads. This isn't a Borstal, Headmaster. What is there to escape from?"

"That's what we have to find out."

Sherborne's tetchiness began bordering on belligerence. "I may be *in loco parentis*, but I'm not God the Father. My wife and I have never spared ourselves in caring for the boys. There isn't a better run House in the school. I have been here longer than anyone else. Experience counts for something. Corley couldn't have had better care."

They walked up into the main hallway. Brannigan said, "I'm not criticising you. If he's gone, he had a reason for going. It's a pity he didn't confide in you, or Mrs. Sherborne." He remembered Mrs. Sherborne's deafness. Sherborne wasn't a particularly approachable housemaster, from the boys' point of view, and his wife, well-meaning as she undoubtedly was, was hard work getting through to. On the whole she was better than Mollie Robbins in Hammond's. Alison's father would, no doubt, have had no qualms about re-staffing more suitably. The incompetent and the deaf would have been told to quit. Sherborne, at nearly sixty, would have gone too, of course. In the few minutes it took to cross the main hall and go into his study he had re-staffed the school in his mind with the young, the brilliant, and the caring. In his pipe-dream there was always money to pay them, and the school building itself rose strong and uncracked on solid un-subsiding foundations.

He sat behind his desk and made Sherborne go through it again.

"Did he leave a note?"

"No."

"Did he get into the locker room to get his suitcase?"

"I hadn't thought of looking."

Well, bloody look, Brannigan thought, but phrased it more politely.

He called in all the housemasters and the senior prefects and sent them to search the school and the grounds. In the meantime Sherborne returned to say that he had left without his suitcase. "All his clothes are here — except his daytime clothes and his mack. He left his bed unmade. It's quite likely he's hiding somewhere in the grounds." His voice, rough with anxiety, spoke without conviction.

"Why, should he do that?"

"Why do small boys do anything?"

"He's eleven. Not an infant. Old enough to reason out his actions."

Sherborne felt a vascular pain in the back of his left leg and was forced to take the nearest chair and sit for a few minutes. When the pain eased he reminded Brannigan that Durrant had gone home twice without reason. "Nobody bullied him."

Brannigan thought, nobody would dare, but didn't voice it. Durrant was a step outside the circle and always would be. Corley was an ordinary, normal, small boy.

David Fleming had been an ordinary, normal, small boy.

Had been.

The anxiety that had been building up like water against a dam began treacherously to break through. He forced himself to contain it.

The search parties returned in half an hour without success.

At nine-fifteen he put a call through to Corley's father at Bridgwater. Alison came into his study and sat in the chair in the window recess as he made it. Blame the boy, she willed him silently. Don't break the news so gently, so defensively.

Let your anger come up. The boy betrays you, not you the boy. He's lucky to have the chance to be here. If he throws that chance back at you then he's a stupid, idiotic, little brat. My father would have taken the hide off him, but you won't, will you — if he's caught. You'll speak sweet reason at him, as you do with all of them. You're soft — that's your trouble. You can't run a school like a young ladies' dancing academy, or a nursing home. Pity is your undoing. Why pity anyone? No-one pities you . . . The words hurtled through her mind so that she couldn't hear what Brannigan was saying and then she forced herself to listen.

He was still apologising, still soothing. "Try not to worry. Boys sometimes act on impulse — perhaps a row with another lad — I don't know . . . Yes, of course I intend calling in the police . . . No, I don't think it would be wise of you to come over. He probably hasn't got very far, but there's always the chance he's making for home. You'd be wiser to stay there and let me know when he arrives . . . Yes, naturally, I'll keep you informed. I'm sorry I had to give you such disturbing news. It will be good news soon, I hope . . . Yes, I agree, he's a very level-headed, pleasant child . . . No, I'm sure he wouldn't have left without a reason . . . I assure . . . Naturally, you're upset . . . Try to keep calm about it for the lad's sake . . . When he does turn up keep it in a low key . . . Give my regards and sympathy to Mrs. Corley and assure her that everything is being done to find the boy . . . to find Neville."

He put the phone down, sweating slightly. He had juggled the conversation, carefully avoiding using the lad's name until Corley senior had mentioned it. Neville. The name had escaped his mind. It didn't speak so highly of the quality of care when a lad's christian name was as elusive as a dandelion seed on the breeze.

He wished Alison would stop looking at him like that. She made him feel like Uriah Heep. What did she expect him to do — beat his jackboots with a horsewhip while breaking the news?

"And now — what?" she asked tiredly. "The police?"

"The police — and afterwards Colonel Goldthorpe."

"And the rest of the governors, too, I suppose? It's like living in the days of the inquisition. Why drag them into' it?'

"It's better they should hear about it directly from me."

"It's better no-one should hear about it at all. You could have waited another hour before telling the boy's father — before calling in the police."

He held on to his patience. "A child is missing — a child is at risk."

"And the school is at risk. It has been ever since the Fleming child died."

He ignored her and began dialling the number of Marristone police station. Detective Inspector Grant came on the line and from him he at last got the support he needed. The school would be searched — this time professionally — and the surrounding countryside would be searched. All patrols would be alerted as soon as he had personal details of the lad. He would be up at the school in fifteen minutes. In cases like these the child was usually found quite quickly. He made it sound very easy and ordinary. Brannigan imagined a Pied Piper line of young Corleys making their way through the countryside and coming up against Grant's substantial midriff one by one.

He had been very cool and phlegmatic about David Fleming, too. That time he had been presented with a *fait accompli* — this time there was a chance of doing something about it.

As soon as he put the phone down it rang again almost immediately.

"Is that the headmaster, Mr. Brannigan?"

"Yes." He thought it was Mrs. Corley and felt a lurch of

104

dismay. Speaking to the lad's father had been bad enough.

"This is Lorena Durrant — Steven's mother." The raucous voice should have been familiar and now that he heard it again it jogged his memory of several irritating conversations he had had with her in the past.

"Good morning, Mrs. Durrant."

His eyes met Alison's and for the first time that day sympathy was mutual.

"Good morning." She pushed out the greeting as if she were dropping a wasp through a window, and then got on quickly with what she had to say. "It was my birthday on Tuesday. I had a most extraordinary present from Steven. I really can't get over it."

Jesus God, Brannigan thought, she's on about the Keats. He remembered Durrant's embarrassment as he had stood at the study door and asked for permission to go down to the town to buy it. Why in the name of sanity was she ringing him up to complain about it? Especially now.

He tried not to speak irritably, but failed. "Some people like that sort of thing. The boy was trying to please you."

"Oh, so you knew about it, then? I thought perhaps you did."

"Yes — he asked my permission to go down to the town to buy it."

The words, like bullets leaving a gun-barrel, cracked out sharply, "And where did he get the money from, Mr. Brannigan? Answer me that?"

She was using up valuable telephone time and he was tempted to put the phone down, but if he did she would ring him back and keep ringing him back.

"I'm busy, Mrs. Durrant. Do you think you could come to the point?"

"The point — oh yes, Mr. Brannigan, I can come to the point. The point is the amount of money my husband sends to Steven — and doesn't send to me. What is he trying to do — buy the boy's affection? Inveigle him away from me?"

Brannigan, at a loss, waited. There was no affection from either parent, and there wasn't much in the way of money either. Durrant senior gave the boy mighty little in either hard cash or fatherly interest.

Not getting a response, she went on. "At first I didn't think anything of it. I'm not well up in these things. And then one of my friends saw it and read the name on it. Would it surprise you to know that it didn't cost Steven a penny less than eighty pounds?"

It surprised Brannigan very much. The woman must be mad. The local bookshop didn't go in for first editions.

He spoke mildly, "Your friend must have misled you. Steven spent less than five pounds."

"Not on that camera, he didn't. My friend's an expert. He's done model photography for the high quality artistic market. If Steven's father is giving him that sort of pocket money then he's earning a sight more than he tells me he's earning."

Brannigan, about to say it wasn't a camera, stopped himself. If she said it was, then it was. Even Durrant would know better than to send his mother a book of love poems — but why tell him he was going out to buy a book of Keats when he wasn't? And where did he get the money from? Obviously if not from his mother then from his father. His father might have had a win on the horses or something. But if he had he wouldn't send it to the boy. Or would he? Hammond might know. As housemaster he was responsible for the boys' money.

He told Mrs. Durrant he would put her through to Hammond and then remembered that Hammond was taking a class. "Or rather — I'll ask him to call you back as soon as he's free."

"And I want to talk to Steven, too."

"Naturally. I'll arrange that as well."

It was after he put the phone down that he remembered that Durrant had come to ask him for the money — and that he had given him six pounds. Eighty? The silly woman was sleeping with a porn photographer who was either cretinous or as high as a kite.

Alison asked, "What was that all about?"

"Rubbish. Lorena Durrant's bed companion is a crass idiot."

"It's a pity," Alison said, "that you can't use that tone of voice all the time."

After the police had come and gone and left him with the feeling that he could lean back against a solid, professional and very comforting wall, Goldthorpe came and effectively kicked it away again. He spoke much as Alison had spoken and told him he should get in touch with Lessing forthwith. He had even used the word 'forthwith'. 'Substantial financial loss" occurred frequently, too. David Fleming's death was a wounding — Corley's disappearance a possible death-blow. Brannigan, tiring of him, told him crisply that his military metaphors were completely out of place. A child had disappeared; he was concerned for the safety of that child. At this moment his concern was focussed there and nowhere else.

Goldthorpe, surprised, climbed down a little. "All the same, it would do no harm to have Lessing up here, Head-master. As an old boy, he has the welfare of the school very much at heart."

"And I haven't — is that what you're implying?"

Goldthorpe took his leave huffily. "I'm not implying anything of the sort. What a ridiculous thing to say! I'll be in touch with you again when you're calmer."

Brannigan saw Goldthorpe to the door and noticed before closing it that Jenny was on her way to the stairs. He

107

called after her. "Nurse Renshaw — could you give me a moment or two please?"

"Yes, of course." She had been informed about Corley's disappearance and was as worried as he was. She said impulsively, "I'm terribly sorry. I know what you're feeling."

He told her to sit down. "Jenny — do you know Corley's christian name?"

The question surprised her. "Yes — don't you? It's Neville."

"You didn't even have to think about it, did you?"

She didn't understand where the question was leading and he didn't explain.

He said, "He's a small red-headed child of eleven with buck teeth and a Somerset accent — I'm right, am I not?"

"You're right."

He had put the child's face together slowly in his mind after going through a mental putting-together of all the other children in his House — like a slowly-formed identikit picture Corley had finally emerged. A school photograph that Sherborne had unearthed had confirmed it. The police were working from the photograph.

"You know the lads pretty well, Jenny."

"I've had most of them in the infirmary at one time or another."

"Tell me about Corley." He corrected himself. "Tell me about Neville."

The question found an echo in her mind. Tell me about David.

She answered thoughtfully. "He's introverted. A worrier. He says he's fine when he isn't because he's scared he'll be told he's worse than he is." She paused wondering if that made sense and decided it did. She tried to clarify it more. "When I took his temperature once I caught him putting the thermometer in a glass of cold water before handing it to me."

"So what do we deduce from that? That he wouldn't go to anyone for help . . . not even to you?"

"I don't know if he needed help. If he did, he didn't come to me."

"Have you heard anything from any of the other boys about him?"

"No. He was a loner. He'd carry whatever it was by himself."

"I see." He sat back in his chair and looked at her. "And now tell me about Fleming — Fleming senior."

She looked away from him. "I don't know what you mean."

"Jenny — you're living in a small community within a small town. The wife of one of the housemasters told me she saw you in a blue car with John Fleming the night before last." He hoped she wouldn't guess that the wife of the housemaster was Alison. Alison had gone on about the undesirability of a member of staff associating with Fleming "as he's so damnably hostile". He had irritated her by answering lightly that these days collaborators didn't have their heads shorn.

Jenny, knowing full well that it was Alison, decided not to say so. Brannigan was suffering enough.

"Are you forbidding me to see John Fleming?"

He knew it wouldn't make any difference if he did. "No. You're free to do as you like — and to see your loyalties whichever way you want to see them."

"Loyalties aren't flags you carry, one in each hand. I'd do everything I could to help him. If the school is to blame for anything, you wouldn't hide it. If I thought differently I would have resigned long ago."

He took it for the compliment it was and was grateful.

She said, sensing that the time was right to ask it, "I should like to have time off to be at the inquest tomorrow afternoon."

He could see that she was stiffening into a defensive attitude expecting him to refuse.

"Of course you may go. Alison will be sitting on her own while I give evidence. I can't persuade her not to attend. She's extremely nervous and worried. Your being with her will help."

To hold Alison's hand hadn't been her intention, but there was no way out of it.

He told her that Lessing was representing the school. "And I'm told there's to be a jury." Lessing had told him this. "Seven local tradesmen," Lessing had said, "all rooting for the Grange. They feed it, they plumb it, they paint it and they wash its windows. They're not likely to pull the plug out." Brannigan had commented acidly on Lessing's code of ethics and Lessing had taken it for the joke it wasn't.

A couple of hours later, during lunchtime, Lessing arrived at the school house. He walked straight through into the dining room, meeting Alison in the doorway as she was on her way to the kitchen to fetch the coffee. She offered him some, but he declined. "I can't stay. I have an appointment with a client in twenty minutes."

After she was out of earshot he said aggrievedly to Brannigan, "You should have informed me, you know."

"I gather Goldthorpe did?"

"Yes — but after I'd heard it in the town first."

"Damn!" Brannigan made a fist of his right hand and then uncurled his fingers slowly. Where gossip was concerned the school was like water running through a colander.

Lessing shrugged. "The place is crawling with police. What do you expect? . . . Any news of the lad yet?"

"No." He had been ringing the police station every hour on the hour and Corley's father had been ringing him at even more frequent intervals. The phone bell was like the rubbing away of insulating tape over an electric wire. He wondered if the child would be found before his own personal flashpoint seared his control.

Lessing said, "Sit down. I have something to say to you. It isn't pleasant."

Brannigan's face seemed visibly to thin so that the bones were prominent. "Go on."

"I think the child who's disappeared had good reason to disappear — if he's the child I saw here the other day."

"Describe him."

"About ten or eleven, small build, red hair. He had been frightened to the point of throwing up." He went on to tell Brannigan about the boy running from the direction of the hollow. "I went to investigate, but I saw no-one. I have no doubt at all that there was someone there. Does the description fit the boy who's gone?"

"Yes."

"Then you've a problem on your hands — a nasty one. I didn't tell you because you've worry enough with the Fleming case. I intended telling you after the inquest. That was a misjudgment on my part. I'm sorry."

Brannigan said heavily, "Obviously there was a reason for his going. It's not pleasant having it confirmed. You say he vomited?"

"Yes — with fright. And his hands had been tied. He managed to loosen the knot." He didn't add that he had dropped the tie in the bushes — a temporary tidying away of a disturbing situation. "It's more than normal bullying. I thought you were fussing too much over Fleming's accident. Now I'm not at all sure that it was an accident. I won't say so at the inquest, of course, but I'm telling you. *Praemonitus, praemunitus.* Forewarned is forearmed. You see, I haven't forgotten my Latin." He smiled wetly, but with genuine sympathy. "Damned good school this."

Alison waited until he had gone before returning. "What did he want?"

111

He decided not to tell her. "He'd heard about Corley — through Goldthorpe."

"And by the look of you made you see how serious it is. The school's good name is being ruined by an irresponsible little brat . . . Where are you going?" He was walking over to the door.

He nearly said, To breathe — to get away from you. "To my study. Durrant can make his phone call to his mother from there."

"Durrant? You're bothered about Durrant — now? At a time like this?"

Yes, he thought, he was particularly bothered about Durrant at a time like this.

He sent for Hammond first. He had asked him to make the phone call as quickly as he could. "Or she'll keep hogging the line." He hadn't bothered asking him the result of it. He asked him now.

Hammond said mildly, "She's crazy. I told her the boy had started the term with eight pounds in his account — and that if any more money had come through he would have given it to me to bank for him. She wanted to know if I opened his letters. I said my duties here were to teach not to run a censorship department."

Unwise, Brannigan thought, but didn't blame him.

"She didn't take that kindly. She even had the gall to talk about a moral duty to open his letters. Moral duty! Mrs. Durrant!" It was the only funny thing that had happened to him for days.

"And then?"

"And then one of the new lads — Wilkinson — ran down the corridor in a pair of football boots, with one of the other lads after him. You know the rule about that. He dislodged a piece of parquet — the bit that's just been repaired where the damp was getting through."

"And you cut Mrs. Durrant off and attended to it."

"Quite."

"Do you think the lad's father sent him any money?"

"No, Headmaster. Do you?"

"No," Brannigan said, "I don't. But I intend asking him about it."

It took Hammond nearly half an hour to find Durrant and in that time Brannigan got through to the police again. There was still no news of Corley. Minutes afterwards Corley's father rang Brannigan. He had no news either and his tension was coming out as barely concealed aggression. Brannigan listened to his criticisms tiredly. On the whole, he thought, they were just. At that moment he would have gladly handed over the school to Corley's father and told him to run it — just to see how easy it was. He had a vision of a bothy in Scotland set miles from anywhere with not a single human being in sight.

Durrant knocked at the door and came in. "You want to see me, sir?"

In some odd way some of the boy's obsequiousness had gone. He had never exactly grovelled before Brannigan, but he had tended to stoop and mumble. Brannigan, catching a look from the boy's eyes, felt uncomfortably as if he were being measured up and found wanting. It was a familiar enough look from Alison — especially during the last few days — but he had never noticed it in Durrant before.

He came crisply to the point. "How much money did you spend on your mother's camera, Durrant?"

The question visibly took the boy off-balance. "What do you mean, sir? What camera?"

"Don't stall. I haven't time for that. The camera you gave her for her birthday. It was to have been a book of Keats — obviously you changed your mind."

Durrant lost an inch or two. "Not very much, sir. I had meant to buy her the book of poems, sir. But I saw the camera in Franklin's — the nearly new shop at the corner of Brook Street."

"How much did you give for it?"

"Four pounds fifty." His voice became ingratiating. "And then I bought the razor, sir. The one you told me to buy." He rubbed his chin. "It does a good job, sir."

"Have you a receipt?"

"For the razor?" He saw Brannigan's expression and went on hastily, "For the camera? Yes, sir, I did have a receipt. But I don't keep them, not unless they're for a lot of money. I threw it away."

"Have you a lot of money? From your father — for instance?"

Durrant's surprise was genuine — so much so that he didn't answer. He seemed to be casting around in his mind for the reason behind such a stupid question. At last he thought he'd found it. "That money you advanced me, sir. You did get it back, didn't you? I told Mr. Hammond about it and asked him to give it back to you."

"Yes, I did get it back. Have you had a substantial sum of money from anyone recently?"

"Chance would be a fine . . ." Again he caught Brannigan's eye. "No, sir."

"Your mother seems to think you have. She phoned me this morning and wants to speak to you. You might as well make the phone call now." He indicated the brown leather armchair. "Go and sit over there and take the phone with you. I have this paper-work to see to." He implied that Durrant would disturb him less if he didn't make the phone call at the desk. Durrant hesitated. Brannigan lied irritably, "I won't listen."

As Durrant picked up the telephone and began to dial, Brannigan noticed his hands for the first time. They were large and bony with prominent knuckles. The nails were well shaped and well kept. Somehow he had expected them

114

to be bitten to the quick. His overall appearance was scruffy, but that was mainly due to the way his hair grew over his collar and to the side-burns the razor had carefully avoided. He looked a strong young brute, but a strong young brute who showered daily without being told. He was a child in a man's body — but some of the time not a child at all.

He was a child now.

His whole attitude as he got through to his mother dropped years off him. His obvious delight as he heard her voice showed in the slight flush in his cheeks and in the relaxing of his attitude. He sat more comfortably in the chair, cradling the telephone base on his knee, stroking the flex absently with his left hand.

"Many happy returns for Tuesday. Did you like my card? And the present?"

Brannigan couldn't hear Lorena Durrant's side of the conversation, but he could see the effect of it. It was as if a cold, unexpected wind had caught the boy naked. His hand on the flex became still.

"What do you mean . . . my father? . . . Why should he? . . . What friend? . . . I don't think I know that friend (there was ice in his own voice now) . . . How would your friend know? . . . Eighty pounds (genuine surprise) . . . You think I spent eighty pounds? . . . If I had it, then I would — on you."

Brannigan looked away.

Durrant said bleakly, "No, I don't see my father much . . . No, he doesn't write much — and you don't either . . . I'm not changing the subject . . . If you want to believe your friend and not me . . . (A long unintelligible tirade which seemed to drive needles into Durrant's skin and leave small flushed areas of distress on his face) . . . All right, I know . . . I'm not criticising . . . Yes, you must have someone . . . I know you do . . . I wasn't trying to . . . It was just a present I thought you'd like . . . I'm sorry you don't like it . . . Why

115

keep on about that? I know money's important . . . Yes, I will tell my father if he . . . No, I'm not lying about that . . . I haven't any . . . If I had I'd let you . . ." (the voice becoming dry, the words difficult to form).

Brannigan looked back at him. The boy's face was set hard as if against the pain of a dental drill. Durrant was the first to hang up. He put the phone down because he couldn't take any more. He got up slowly and took it over to the desk. He looked at Brannigan as if he were an apparition at the end of a long tunnel. And then he knew him.

"Thank you, sir."

Brannigan said gently, "Women — mothers included — are creatures of many moods. She probably liked your present very much. Someone misled her about the price — that's all."

He had intended asking Durrant about Corley, but couldn't. It would be like putting the boot in after his mother's vicious heels had trodden all over him.

Durrant went straight from Brannigan's study to the store-room off the gym. The sun slanting down from the high window warmed the pile of new coir mats so that they smelt and looked like gingerbread. They were the only new items in the place. He pulled a couple of them into a corner behind the door and sat down. He couldn't face anybody yet. Brannigan's last few words were like fire in his chest. He was as near to tears as he had ever been.

Damn his mother, damn his bloody mother. And then because that was too unbearable he switched his mind off her completely and let the force of his pain and rage fall on the man she was with. A photographer. A mincing, mealy-mouthed, misinformed, shitting photographer. Eighty pounds! If Corley's camera had been worth eighty pounds Corley wouldn't have handed it over so easily. Anyway — who would give a kid of ten, or whatever he was, a camera

116

worth that much? What sort of daft parents would do a thing like that? What was Corley's old man — a bank-manager or bloody Croesus?

He regretted now that he had gone to Brannigan for the postage money. If he hadn't he couldn't have posted the bloody thing. A fiver for a Keats had seemed a nice round sum and a bit of a joke, too. It wasn't a joke any more. It would be even less of a joke if Corley split on him.

He wondered where Corley had gone. If he was aiming for home, then a kid with any intelligence would have arrived there by now. It had rained during the night. If he had been out in that, the cold and wet would probably kill him. His chest rattled when he breathed — or perhaps he just breathed oddly. When he'd held him down in the hollow his breath had squeaked out of him like rusty bellows and his lips had turned blue. It had been disgusting of him to get sick all over him.

The memory was unpleasant and he switched it off.

He began building an image of the photographer in his mind. He saw him as small, fat and frightened, but getting no satisfaction from that began building him bigger. An enemy had to be worthy of him. Fleming's father was worthy of him. His hatred made him ten feet tall. He tried making the photographer ten feet tall, but the imagery wouldn't work. He kept seeing him as small, fat and greasy, lying naked in bed with his mother. Despatching him would be like killing a pig. The blood would get on his mother and defile her. His inability at this moment to control his fantasies frightened him. He had always, until now, been able to walk the particular corridor in his mind he chose to walk. His own feeling of supremacy had never been shaken. Now he felt used — as if other hands were controlling the power-house and he couldn't pull them away.

There was someone crossing the floor of the gym and he sat quietly willing whoever it was to go away.

A small dark-haired boy with eyes as brown as pennies came and stood at the door. He hadn't seen this one before — or if he had he hadn't noticed him. He looked about seven.

"Excuse me . . ." The voice was high-pitched — very well bred. His mother would have mocked it as very "refained."

"Scarper!"

The boy looked as if he had heard, but didn't believe what he had heard. "I've come to fetch a rounders ball for Mr. Innis. I think I can see them in that basket over there."

He began treading delicately over Durrant's outstretched leg. Durrant raised it, tripping him. He came down heavily on his hands. His lips trembled. "I really can't go without it."

"No, you really can't, can you? Perhaps now you're here you can't go at all." Durrant felt his dark mood lighten. "What's your name?"

The child, as still as a spider that is being watched from a vast distance by someone with a huge death-dealing foot, took a minute or two to answer. "Peter."

"You're not Peter here. You won't be Peter any more until you leave. What's your other name?"

"Christopher."

"Peter Christopher — what?"

"Nothing. Peter Christopher. My father owns the Christopher Potteries in Stoke."

"Oh, he does, does he? And what does he make in his pottery — piss-pots?"

The fair skin flushed. "He makes the best dinner services and tea sets in the world."

"He's rich — your old man?"

It was not done to speak about money. "I really don't know."

"You really don't know! You really aren't very bright,

are you?" Durrant leaned over and pushed back the grey flannel cuff from the child's left wrist. He looked in disgust at the Mickey Mouse watch. "Is that the best your old man can give you?"

The tears were near the surface. "I like it."

"That's what I mean — you're dim."

"Mr. Innis will be wanting the ball . . . I really must get it."

Durrant raised his leg as a barrier. "I haven't finished talking to you yet. What did your old man give you for your birthday — a toy duck to put in your bath?"

"As a matter of fact," with great dignity, "he gave me a horse — a real one."

"Oh, I say — now isn't that something! So that piss-pot factory makes bread, does it?"

"I have already told you my father makes . . ."

"Piss-pots. You've ears like piss-pot handles, did you know that?" Durrant got on his knees and pressed the boy's ears back against his skull. "That's how they should be — flat."

"You're hurting me." As the ears whitened under pressure the child's eyes became bloodshot with tears. Fascinated, Durrant pressed harder and the tears spurted out and trickled down the sides of the tightly closed mouth. He wondered how hard he would have to press before the mouth gaped open and the kid began to bawl. His own pain was forgotten now and he began to feel euphoric. Dust danced in the beam of sunlight. The skin and gristle under his fingers were like organ notes — press harder and the noise would come.

Innis, at the doorway, snapped, "Durrant!"

Durrant, reorientating gradually, released the pressure and his hands dropped at his side.

The child, aware that the door of the torture chamber was open and that the liberator was beside it, began trembling softly from head to foot.

Innis said gently, "It's all right. Fetch the ball and go."

"Yes, sir."

As the child bent over the ball basket Innis saw that his ears under the fall of dark hair were scarlet. He waited for the child to leave the room before he rounded on Durrant. "What the hell's the matter with you?"

"I don't know what you mean."

"Be at my study tonight at seven sharp — and I'll tell you precisely what I mean."

Durrant's eyes became limpet soft. "Yes, of course I'll be there. What you saw just now might have seemed — well — rather harsh treatment — but the boy's attitude — he . . ."

"Keep your excuses until later. I've a P.E. class outside. Seven o'clock."

"Yes."

"Yes, *sir!*"

Durrant looked at him in mild surprise. "Yes, sir. As you say, sir."

"And get out of here and back to your class."

"I was just about to go, sir."

He moved indolently past Innis and out through the gymnasium. Innis, grim-faced, watched him go.

Eight

FLEMING SPENT TEN minutes at the undertaker's Chapel of Rest and then tried to walk the experience out of his system. The small coffin was on a trestle covered with purple velvet. There was even canned music. It had nothing at all to do with David. He wished he could have some belief in a spirit life. He often had bursts of conversation with David in his head: "It's a posting to Paris. You'd have liked Paris." And now, as he walked the cliff path: "The propellor came off your aeroplane. The wind from the open window caught it. Fragile stuff balsa."

Purple velvet.

Brahms.

Unspoken apologies heavy in the air.

The divorcing of the spirit from the body made thinking about the body possible. He didn't believe in the spirit but he talked to the spirit. Correction . . . he talked to David.

Or he talked to himself.

He wished he could see Shulter again, but didn't want to seek him out. A casual meeting might be helpful, but an arranged meeting at the rectory would be too much like a professional appointment with a doctor or a dentist. Your symptoms, Fleming, are to be expected at this stage of the disease. Take a dose of faith twice a day and the prognosis will improve.

On the way to the undertaker's he had looked in at the church, a red-brick turn-of-the-century building at the corner of Marristone High Street. It had seemed right, mainly for Ruth's sake, to accept Shulter's offer to hold the service there. It was difficult to rationalise his deferring to what he believed would be Ruth's wishes when Ruth was no longer there. Looking inside the church was rather like looking at an execution sword in advance so that familiarity would ease the shock of seeing it on the day. He doubted if he could take the funeral service at all, but so far he had taken everything and survived. There had been a bowl of early summer flowers on the altar and some petunia petals had fallen in an untidy pink pool on the white cloth. The untidiness had made it more acceptable. David had dropped things all over the place, too.

So did Jenny.

Her bedroom would have inspired Herrick to write a poem on it. Sweet disorder. Wild civility. She was as untidy as hell.

When he returned to The Lantern he made a couple of abortive attempts to phone her at the school. Each time the line was engaged. After lunch he drove past her flat in Nelson Street and on impulse stopped and rang the bell. There was no-one in. He remembered she had said she would be on duty. He didn't know what to do with the rest of the afternoon. Time that until now had pushed onwards like an incoming tide seemed sluggishly to reach highwater mark and be still.

He decided to go back to The Lantern and it was there that he ran into the reporter who told him about Corley. It was the same reporter who had written the paragraph in the *Marristone Herald* about David. Their previous meeting hadn't been easy, but this time it was Kenilworth who had news to impart. He waylaid Fleming outside the bar.

"A child has gone missing from the Grange."

"What?" Fleming, still too deep in his own David-orientated world to be able to think of any child outside it, couldn't at first grasp what Kenilworth was saying.

Kenilworth explained patiently. "A young lad, about the same age as your son, has disappeared from the school. A big police search is on. Brannigan won't talk. And I've just had the usual routine stuff from fuzz headquarters. What's your feelings on it — off the record — at least for now?"

Fleming said shortly, "None. What feelings do you expect me to have?" All the same he was shocked and showed it. It was a like a stone being thrown into a pool and causing a new circle within an existing circle. He hoped wherever the child was he was alive and well.

"You've no comment?"

"What do you expect me to say?" (Bully for the lad for getting over the wall in time?)

"You're being very careful, Mr. Fleming." Kenilworth's small blue eyes were regarding him thoughtfully. "I won't land you in a slander action. I know quite well where the line is drawn. But as a father yourself, you'll know what the lad's father is feeling — a comment along those lines wouldn't come amiss."

"What do you want — a statement of sympathy?"

"Something like that."

A lobbying of parents in a massed march of vengeance against the school.

Fleming said, "I'm sorry. You've a job to do and it's not an easy one, but I'm not giving you any quotes."

"And you can't tell me about tomorrow's inquest either?"

"Nothing that you won't pick up for yourself while you're there. You will, of course, attend." It wasn't a question.

"Yes, I'll attend." Kenilworth added, "We may seem a tough bunch professionally but we've youngsters of our own, most of us — not at the Grange, we haven't that sort of salary, and for the first time I'm glad of it. I know how you feel and I know how Corley's father feels. Unfortunately my sympathy carries no weight whatsover." He turned away with a grimace of defeat. No words could be bled out of Fleming now, but there was always tomorrow.

Thirza arrived at The Lantern at a few minutes after five and was told that Fleming had provisionally booked a room for her. She had every intention of staying there no matter what it was like so promptly confirmed the booking.

"Is Mr. Fleming in?"

The reception clerk told her that he was having tea in the residents' lounge on the first floor and directed her there. The lounge, originally a bedroom, had a red flocked paper and was furnished in black imitation leather. Its narrow bay window faced the sea. Fleming, the pot of tea untouched on the small oak table beside him, was standing with his back turned to her looking out.

She said gently, "Hardly my scene — as you said."

Surprised out of his reverie, he turned and smiled at her. "You improve it."

She joined him at the window. "It's a good view — that's its saving grace, I suppose?"

"That and the beer. Now you've seen it, will you stay?"

"I'll stay." She slipped her hand through his arm. "Why order tea if you don't intend drinking it?"

"I forgot about it. It's the only room here with a television set. I'm hoping to catch the local news." He told her about Corley.

She had spent part of the day finding out all the relevant information about the inquest. That Lessing was an old boy of the school hadn't surprised her. Robert Breddon, the coroner, hadn't let it out, but she had other sources. She was pretty sure that all the inquest would produce would be a statement of identification — a few general questions — and a verdict of accidental death. If John wanted to fight for damages and kill the school in so doing then she would take the battle on, but only if there was the slightest chance of winning it. She didn't think there was. Her own fees she would gladly waive, but litigation was an expensive business. She had never believed in pouring money away in a lost cause. She asked him about the child who had gone missing.

"He's about David's age,"

"Do you know anything else about him?"

"No."

She looked at him astutely, "You see it as more ammunition?"

"It could be. Let's hope he doesn't end up as David ended up."

She was relieved that he was able to get down to basics. At times they both found it extraordinarily difficult to talk to each other.

They sat and watched the local news. Corley wasn't mentioned at all. She got up and switched off the television. "It's probably rather soon. Lots of children go missing. They don't hit the headlines for a day or two."

It was his suggestion that they should go for a walk before dinner and while she was up in her bedroom changing her shoes he phoned the school again. This time he got through to someone who sounded like Alison Brannigan, but could have been a school secretary if Brannigan ran to one. He gave his name and asked for Jenny. The voice told him to hold the line and at the end of five minutes said that she couldn't be located. He asked if the missing boy had been found. The silence was almost palpable for a minute or two and then the receiver was replaced. An outright no would have been more sensible. Brannigan, he thought, was cursed with a stupid wife.

Jenny, who could quite easily have been found if Alison had bothered to look, phoned The Lantern herself an hour later and was told by the reception clerk that Fleming was out, but had booked in for dinner. "Have you a message?"

Jenny said she hadn't.

She wanted to meet him. He was in her mind all the time. She wasn't entitled to any time off, but Mollie would cover for her for an hour. In the last few days Mollie had become pathetically keen to seem as efficient as possible. She told her she was going out — but not for long. "The infirmary is empty. If Neville shows up and I'm needed you can get me at The Lantern."

Mollie asked dryly, "Booze or Fleming?"

"So the grape-vine flourishes."

"In this hot-house atmosphere, dear, what do you expect? And the lesser of two evils is booze."

Jenny forgave her. John had given her a rough ride and her seat on the saddle was still precarious.

Dinner at The Lantern was served from seven onwards. Jenny, still in her matron's uniform, arrived at seven-thirty. They were in the middle of the fish course. His woman, whoever she was, was dressed in deep blue and the highlights in her hair were silver. Waves of jealousy bordering on pure and simple hate tingled through her like electric shocks.

Thirza said quietly, "There's a girl with red hair and murder in her eyes willing me dead. She's standing in the doorway."

Fleming glanced over his shoulder and then, forgetting to apologise to Thirza, got up quickly and went over to her.

His delight in seeing her halted her exit. "Jenny! I've been trying to get you all day."

She didn't believe him.

"Your school phone was in continuous use. When I did get through you weren't to be found."

"I was there." Her underlip was thrust out sulkily like a child's.

"And you're here now. We've only just started dinner. You must join us."

"Dressed like this — and join who?"

"Thirza Crayshaw — an old family friend, the solicitor who's representing me at the inquest."

Thirza, watching, thought, so that's the one, and was surprised. The hurt and the pain had rolled off him like a cloud melting in the sun as he saw her and spoke to her. The only thing she obviously had in her favour was youth — and that wasn't always an asset. Her uniform dress was ridiculous, it even had cuffs. There were belt slots, but no belt. She had the freckles that went with red hair and hadn't bothered to disguise them. She didn't bother to disguise her feelings either. She had the look of a betrayed lover who was being gradually coaxed to a state of faith.

She wasn't sure of him.

Nor he of her.

So they hadn't known each other long.

The affair was at the delicate perimeter of what could be a deep and healing permanency — or just transient. Whichever way it went his response at this moment was good to see.

I lay no claim, she told Jenny silently. Lay him and claim him and make him normal again — if you can. And good luck to you.

Jenny had arrived at The Lantern believing she could eat a substantial meal if offered one, but she discovered when she sat down at the table that she could scarcely eat at all. Thirza, adroit at the social graces, kept up the necessary patter of conversation. Threesomes — even this particularly awkward threesome — she had always been able to handle. Closer relationships eluded her.

It was over coffee that the first reference to Corley was made.

Fleming asked abruptly, "Why did he go?"

Jenny, carefully spooning brown sugar into a cup that was too small, said "Neville? . . . I don't know."

"No — Corley. The lad from the school."

"Neville Corley. If he had a brother he would be Corley Minor. If he were one of three then I don't know what he'd be — perhaps Corley subminor." She was talking nonsense and knew it. Thirza had badly upset her, just by being there and looking as she did.

Thirza observed unnecessarily, "You don't approve of the British public school."

"I don't approve of depersonalising children."

Thirza tried to draw her out. "Speaking generally, it can't be a bad system. Of course there are pockets of disaster —

the Grange is probably one of them. The fault is usually at the top — what's the head like?"

Jenny put her cup down untouched. "Caring."

Once spoken she considered it and believed it to be true. Within his personal limitations, Brannigan was caring.

Thirza pursued it. "Then — weak?"

Jenny thought, If you weren't batting on John's side our conversation would end now. As it was she considered the question for some while before answering. "It's a great deal easier to be tough and single-minded than it is to be open-minded and fair. The head before him, so I'm told, was brilliant. I think that means he was as thick as a board and doled out punishment like an army sergeant major."

She looked at Fleming to see how he had taken her defence of Brannigan.

"Strength and brutality," he pointed out, "are two different things. If you captain a ship, you give the orders and the crew obeys them. If there's unrest you look into it and act. You say Brannigan is caring. It takes a stronger quality than care alone to keep a ship on an even keel. He should have known the rot was setting in — he should have located it and stopped it. If he had, David might have been alive." He was aware himself that he had said 'might have been' rather than 'would have been'.

Jenny drank her coffee quickly. She had already over-stayed the hour. Fleming went out to the car with her. "I'm glad you came. I wish you could have stayed."

"Mollie Robbins is standing in for me."

"You mean she's sitting in her room with her head-phones on like a female Nero while the school burns." He opened the car door for her.

She got in and rolled down the window. "Have you ever thought what would happen to her if Brannigan ditched her?"

"No. But I'll think about it now. Frankly, I don't give a

damn and neither should Brannigan — the lads should come first."

She said curtly, "You'd make a splendid headmaster."

He was surprised into laughter. She was being moody and cantankerous and he knew the reason why. He lifted her hand off the wheel and held it in both of his. "I'm sorry Thirza spoilt our meal. I'm sorry you ate hardly any of it. She's decorative, and pleasant, and kind. Ruth was fond of her and so am I. Tomorrow at the inquest she'll do all she can. Tonight we'll sleep in our separate beds." He kissed her fingers gently and replaced her hand on the wheel. It occurred to him that this would be their last meeting before the inquest, but didn't mention it. Her attitude to the school was ambivalent and that was to be expected.

Jenny drove back to the Grange in a state of growing depression. Her jealousy of Thirza was as difficult to throw off as would be an invasion of persistent leeches. He might not sleep with her tonight, but there would be other nights. Any sexual dance with Thirza would be a slow and graceful pavane followed by a cool and lengthy disrobing — not a mad sprawl of tears and anger followed by an exquisite orgasmic burst of pleasure that her body having once known couldn't forget. She kept wanting him. She wanted him now.

She went up to the treatment room where she had left Mollie and found her putting wads of blood-soaked cotton wool into the waste-bin.

"For God's sake — what happened?"

Mollie, sweating slightly, managed a smile. "Young Carson tripped and banged his nose on the edge of his bed. I coped. He's all right." She added unnecessarily, "There was a gory mess."

"So I see. Did you let him stay in the infirmary."

"No — he's back in the dormitory."

"It's as well to keep an eye on him — at least for a while. By the look of that it's recent."

"Not that recent — I just didn't get around to clearing up." Her fat cheeks broke into a sudden smile giving her face an unexpected look of genuine pleasure. "Corley's home and dry."

Jenny's mood swung upwards. "When?"

"Some time this evening. Bridgwater via Birmingham. He needs to swot up his geography — or perhaps he was just unlucky with his hitches. According to Hammond, Brannigan got the news through the police."

"Not through his father?"

"No . . . I'm just telling you what Hammond told me. According to Hammond, Corley senior is nursing a pretty big grievance. He won't communicate with the school until he gets a coherent story out of his son. There won't be any marching back of the penitent . . . at least not yet."

Jenny absently picked up a bottle of surgical spirit and dampened a piece of wool with it. There were blood stains on the table. "Is he all right?"

"Yes, as far as we know. The police didn't say he wasn't."

After Mollie had left the room, Jenny put a call through to Fleming. He was surprised and pleased to hear her voice again so soon.

"You're phoning to tell me you have the night off after all?"

"No. I'm phoning to tell you that Neville Corley is safely home."

"I see. I'm glad." She knew that he spoke out of a depth of feeling.

"I knew you would be. I couldn't let the night pass without letting you know."

"Why did he leave — do you know that now?"

"No. All I know is he's home."

And David, she thought, will never be home.

For the first time that evening her gentleness broke through the protective crust of aggression.

"John . . . I mind about you . . . very deeply."

Afraid of a silence that might grow — or an answer that might be forced and artificial — she put the phone down.

He had already experienced the difficulty of contacting her, so didn't try to ring her back. He had a lot to say. Or perhaps not so much — just a word or two that mattered. Mind. A deceptively mild word. He could think of others.

Nine

THE CORONER'S COURT was held in a room in the local police station. The police station, barely ten years old, had a reception hall that wouldn't have shamed a four-star hotel. The floor was terrazzo-tiled and decorated with potted plants. The enquiry desk, manned by the station sergeant, was of best quality teak.

Robert Breddon thought with some nostalgia of the room in the town hall where all the earlier inquests had been held. This place, the product of the affluent sixties, put him in mind of a tarted-up pub. The floor was damn slippy too, he always felt he had to pick his way across it with extreme caution. He had been coroner now for over twenty years, but couldn't learn to like the job. An essential part of it was to view the dead bodies, and most of them turned his stomach. There were a lot of drownings along the coast and some of them had been in the sea a long time. Identification — another essential part of the job — wasn't always easy for the relatives. Road accidents were almost worse. He never ceased to be shocked by what a steering-wheel and shattered

131

glass could do to human flesh. This case, today, saddened him, as all cases involving children did. The Fleming child had been almost unmarked. His light had gone out with no visible brutality. At the mortuary he had looked asleep.

As was his practice he kept away from the court until the last possible moment. In a small town like Marristone Port everyone knew everyone else and it wasn't easy to draw the demarcation line between friendliness and formality. He'd golfed and had drinks with some of the jury, but it would be impossible to whistle up a jury unknown to him. Lessing, he believed, was sufficiently professional to act in a professional manner, and so were the police, but he couldn't vouch for anyone else. The courtroom at ten minutes to two was almost full. The public tended as a rule to ignore this type of entertainment, but today's inquest was just sufficiently out of the ordinary to pull them in. The major role would be played by Brannigan himself. Lessing would carry him as best he could, but nerves did strange things to people. The blindfold was a complicating factor. Fleming's representative, apart from a brief courtesy call, was an unknown quantity, and Fleming, he'd heard, was out for blood. Before the proceedings got under way he got Lessing to identify Fleming for him and then spoke a few words of sympathy to him.

Fleming inclined his head in acknowledgment. He hadn't known what to expect — certainly not a room like this. There were high windows from floor to ceiling overlooking a small yard. The weather had suddenly become very warm and the too-bright sun was partially screened by long green curtains which cast a green glow over everyone. Even the coroner's white thatch of hair looked green, like a dye gone drastically wrong. He sat up on a dais with his clerk at a table in front of him. The jury were to his right and the witness stand to his left. The green sunlight washed over all.

It was like a film set. He couldn't believe in any of it.

In a moment the cameras would begin to roll and mood music would play. He began to have serious doubts about his sanity. He couldn't recall David at all. He couldn't even conjure up his features.

Thirza said quietly to him. "You're okay." It was a command.

"It's like something shot on a bloody stage. I can't feel David."

She understood his panic. "You probably saw the place quite differently in your mind. It's as real as anything you imagined."

She was aware that Breddon was looking over at her and trying to assess her potential. He would, she hoped, be as professionally objective as he possibly could be. To hope that of the jury would be like hoping for the moon. As for Lessing — she disliked him on sight. He was mentally divesting her, his eyes busy on her breasts.

The proceedings began with the identity of the deceased. Not you, David, Fleming thought as he spoke the few necessary words, the deceased. The place of death came next. The hold of the *Mariana*. Fleming tried to conjure up the memory of it and saw it quite clearly like a sketch in a book. He could neither feel it, nor smell it, nor be appalled by it. It was a hold in a ship — meaningless.

The police evidence was brisk and catalogued events like a railway timetable. They arrived. They saw. They functioned. They departed. The blindfold was mentioned but not stressed.

The pathologist followed the police to the witness stand. He identified himself as Edward Blane and spoke the oath in a sharp, staccato voice. He had, he said, carried out the post-mortem. The coroner asked him to read out his report.

"The only relevant findings at the post-mortem were a contusion of the left forehead without an associated fracture

133

of the skull. There was no significant bleeding into the skin, which suggests that the contusion occurred at the time of death. The cause of death was a fracture dislocation of the second and third cervical vertebrae with compression of the cervical spinal cord."

The coroner looked up from his own copy of the report. "In layman's terms — a broken neck?"

"That is so."

"Go on."

"There was no other evidence of any injury or illness apart from the findings described above."

"Have you anything to add to your report, Dr. Blane?"

"No. The child's neck was broken by the fall. Prior to that he was in a good state of health."

The coroner turned to Lessing. "Do you wish to question the witness?"

Lessing shook his head.

"Miss Crayshaw, is there any question you wish to ask on behalf of Mr. Fleming?"

Thirza stood up. "Please — if I may. Dr. Blane, does your phrase 'any other injury' cover sexual assault?"

"Yes."

"Were you requested to examine the child with that in mind?"

"My examination would have included that — without a request being made."

"But the request was made?"

"Yes — by Dr. Preston."

"There was no evidence of this?"

"As I have stated in my report — no."

Thirza turned to the coroner. "I believe Dr. Preston is being called as a witness?"

"Yes, immediately following Dr. Blane."

"Then that is all I wish to ask this witness. Thank you."

The exchange of question and answer was to Fleming like

the sharp bouncing of a ping-pong ball across a table. He still couldn't connect it with David. That the pathologist's hands had actually touched and explored David's flesh was a fact he could accept intellectually but not emotionally. The post-mortem had seemed more real to him when he had sat at The Lantern with Shulter and had tried to blot it out of his mind. This tall thin man with the staccato voice was as far removed from David as David now was far removed from this green-lit circus.

Dr. Preston was sworn in. He stated that he had seen the body in the hold and had pronounced the child dead. He then went on to report on the removal of the body to the mortuary.

The coroner turned to Thirza again. "You have a question for this witness?"

"Yes, sir." Thirza took the sketch out of her briefcase and requested that it might be passed to Dr. Preston.

The coroner agreed. "But if I see it first, and then Mr. Lessing and the jury, we'll understand where your questions are leading."

The sketch passed from hand to hand. One of the jurors tittered, the rest, together with the coroner himself, looked puzzled. Lessing's glance was brief and dismissive, he looked slightly amused.

Thirza asked, "You've seen this sketch before, Dr. Preston?"

"Yes. In my surgery. The child's father showed it to me."

The coroner interrupted. "Would you describe the drawing to the rest of the court, Dr. Preston, please — and then explain its significance."

Dr. Preston looked down at the sketch and then up from it towards Fleming. He acknowledged him briefly with a little nod of sympathy. "It's a sketch of a caterpillar — a caterpillar hugely out of proportion — on a bed. Under it is written 'Wolly (a child's mis-spelling of

135

Woolly) Bear on D's bed'. It's significance lies in the fact that it's regressive. By that I mean that David Fleming at the age of twelve — within a week or so of his death — drew a picture that was symptomatic of a period of distress he went through at the age of six. At six he awoke alone in a strange room at night and was terrified — the caterpillar was on his face. From then on for a period of two years or so he had nightmares. The caterpillar was the projection of his fear. He drew it to show his state of mind and left the sketches where his parents could find them and tear them up . . . graphic representation of something he couldn't bring himself to speak about." He paused and looked at Fleming. "The child's father could put it better than I can, but that is roughly how he explained it to me."

Thirza said quickly, "I don't think we need ask Mr. Fleming to add to that. You've explained it quite clearly. David drew the sketch as a child of six would draw it. He wrote the words as a child of six would write them. He was twelve and had the intelligence of a twelve-year-old. His other work showed no sign of regression. A shock, either sexual assault, which has been discounted, or some form of intolerable bullying would perhaps result in this sketch. It could have been a cry for help. Would you agree to this, Doctor?"

"It's possible."

"Wouldn't you say probable?"

"I'm not a psychiatrist. I found the sketch disturbing. So much so that I mentioned it to the pathologist. Beyond that, anything I say is conjecture."

The coroner, aware that what should have been a brisk and sympathetic walk from a to be was taking an awkward and unforeseen turn, asked for more clarification. "Are you trying to say that the boy's state of mind was suddenly unbalanced by something — and that his fall might have been deliberate?"

Thirza said, "I saw the hatch to the hold this morning. He couldn't have tripped and fallen — the edge of the hatch came too high. The fact that he wore a blindfold is extremely worrying."

"You're implying suicide?"

"I'm open-minded. The doctor, on his admission, is worried by the sketch."

Lessing was on his feet. "Dr. Preston — I have the greatest regard for your competence as a general pracititioner, but on your own admission your knowledge of psychiatry is slight. Wouldn't you say that only an expert witness in the field of psychiatry would be competent to give an opinion?"

Preston looked at Fleming again. "Unfortunately the child's parents didn't call in a psychiatrist during the early years when the symptoms occurred fairly frequently. This last drawing was after a lapse of time during which the boy had no nightmares. Something triggered it."

Lessing looked at the jury and then at the public in the courtroom. "One of the jurors saw the drawing and laughed — quite honestly, it's a funny picture. The kind of thing a lad might have drawn as a joke. I'm not a psychiatrist — any more than Dr. Preston is a psychiatrist. It didn't strike me, when I saw it just now, as being sinister. Dr. Preston might not have seen it as sinister if the child's father, who was naturally very overwrought, hadn't backed it with lurid tales of long ago . . ."

Fleming's anger until now held in control suddenly burst to the surface. "What the hell are you trying to say — that I'm a liar?"

Thirza said an agonised, "Please!"

The coroner spoke above her. "Mr. Fleming — Miss Crayshaw is representing you here. There are rules of procedure and I can't allow you to disrupt them. Mr. Lessing's turn of phrase was unfortunate. I'm sure as from now he'll choose his words with more care."

Lessing, who had made his point, shrugged slightly and smiled. "All parents here have the greatest sympathy with Mr. Fleming. Bereavement — especially when it's sudden and shocking — tends to colour our judgment. We can't think clearly. We see shadows where they don't exist."

And now, dear Christ, Fleming fumed, he's implying I'm mad. Thirza's eyes held his in warning and heeding her he remained silent.

The coroner suggested dryly that Mr. Lessing might have a question to put to the doctor. Lessing said he had. "Did you treat David Fleming professionally at any time, Dr. Preston?"

"Yes. He had mumps recently."

"Apart from the physical discomfort, did he seem otherwise normal?"

"Yes."

"Not obviously depressed or frightened?"

"During the periods of my visits — no."

"In retrospect, you weren't in the slightest degree worried about him until his father produced this silly sketch?" He corrected himself with a comical side-glance at the coroner intended to be seen by everyone. "I beg your pardon, not the right choice of adjective — let me re-phrase that . . . this disturbing sketch."

There was a titter again from the same juror. The coroner mentally cursed Lessing for playing it the way he was playing it. A child lay dead. The child's father was just a few yards away. In this sort of situation laughter was obscene.

The doctor thought the same. He answered with ill-concealed animosity, but he answered honestly. "I had no reason to feel any concern about his emotional state."

The coroner, quite patently relieved by the answer, was about to dismiss him when Thirza indicated that she had one more question to ask. "Is it true, Doctor, that statistically the number of child suicides has risen dramatically in the last few years?"

The coroner protested before Lessing could. "That's a generalisation, Miss Crayshaw. It isn't relevant."

As Lessing had earlier, she had made her point and was prepared to withdraw gracefully. "I'm sorry. It seemed relevant to me."

Dr. Preston answered her. "I can't quote statistics. You might well be right. The Samaritans have received more distress calls from children in recent years."

The coroner picked up the reins again. "We have to deal with facts — not conjecture. We know the child fell. We know the nature of the injuries which caused his death. We don't know his state of mind. You produced the sketch, Miss Crayshaw, but you haven't explained how it got into Mr. Fleming's possession. Can you tell us that now?"

"David gave it to the school matron." Jenny's surname had gone out of her mind. "The matron gave it to Mr. Fleming."

The coroner knew that the school matron wasn't on the list of witnesses. He could see her at the back of the courtroom sitting with Mrs. Brannigan. Alison Brannigan looked as grimly composed as if she were listening to a case at the Old Bailey. He hadn't met her socially for several months, but she looked years older than she had then. The girl at her side didn't look too well either. Anything she might have to say about handing over the sketch probably wouldn't affect the verdict either way. It was best to let matters lie.

Now that the medical evidence was over, Brannigan himself was the next witness.

He spoke the oath quite firmly. The fact that he was amongst friends was calming. He was careful not to look at Fleming and he was careful, too, not to look at his wife. He reminded himself that he mustn't answer the coroner with too much familiarity — he was Bob Breddon on the golf course and at the Rotary Club, but he wasn't Bob Breddon here. The jurors were, as Lessing had said, very well known to him, too. After a first quick glance at them he hastily looked away. There was a strong bias in his favour and Fleming would be blind not to see it.

The coroner's first question was a gentle leading-in. "As a headmaster of many years experience, Mr. Brannigan, you know the minds of young children rather better than most. Would you say that David Fleming had settled happily into the Grange?"

"I would say so — yes."

"What is your opinion of the sketch he drew?"

Brannigan hesitated. His honest answer would be to say that it worried him in the extreme. But what good would it do? Breddon would ride him with a very easy hand on the reins and the hurdles would be as small as he could make them. If he gave the wrong answer now then this hurdle would be one of many that could bring the school down. One could pay too high a price for a clear conscience. He had a mental image of Alison and one or two of the older members of staff crawling out from under. The child was dead — why hurt them unnecessarily.

"I was perturbed by it. It could mean a lot or it could mean nothing. I didn't dismiss it out of hand, but equally I think it would be foolish to read too much into it. In the teaching profession we're fed a somewhat indigestible diet of psychology. We tend to see the Child Mind in capital letters. We even think we understand it. Children are very diverse creatures — but for the most part they behave quite logically. I believe that if the sketch had been a cry for help it would have been followed by a more practical and under-standable spoken plea for help. The boy would have gone to one of the staff and stated his case."

"And would have been listened to sympathetically?"

"Of course."

"Did you — or any member of your staff — notice any change of mood in the boy recently?"

"No."

"Why do you suppose he had bandaged his eyes before the fall?" He had been about to say accident but checked himself in time.

"I don't know."

"Was he an imaginative child?"

"Yes. He had a flair for visualising scenes. He came up with some good ideas for the school play. He could have been acting out a fantasy at the time of the fall." He caught Lessing's eye. Lessing looked pleased. The coroner showed no emotion whatsoever, but his support was like a strong shorewards current in a treacherous sea.

Fleming thought, "That's right — heel your conscience into the mud, God damn you." A grudging respect that had been growing slowly for Brannigan during the past days was dissipated and became contempt. He wished Thirza would stand up and say something and tried to will her into action but she resolutely kept her face away from him.

The coroner went on quietly. "It's an explanation that seems to me quite feasible — but we're still in the realms of conjecture. I think we should proceed to examine the facts of the case as we know them. As headmaster you sanctioned the visit of the boys to the Maritime Museum?"

"Yes — the responsibility is mine. The boys were working on a shipping project. Last year the school produced work on marine biology. It's my policy to use the environment of the school as fully as possible."

"Did you inspect the Maritime Museum before arranging the boys' visit?"

"Yes. It seemed to me no more hazardous than our visits to the beaches and caves of last year. There is always some danger."

"Quite. It's the degree of reasonable care that counts in a

case of this kind. How many boys were put in the care of one teacher?"

"Eight. The boys ranged in age from eight to sixteen. Their master, Mr. Hammond, is a highly responsible man. I had no qualms whatsoever."

The coroner leaned back in his chair, satisfied. "Mr. Hammond will be our next witness. Before he is called have you anything to ask this witness?" The question was to both Lessing and Thirza. Lessing said no. Brannigan, so far, was doing extremely well. His father-in-law would have been proud of him.

Thirza said, "Yes . . . When you inspected the *Mariana*, Mr. Brannigan, did you notice that one of the hatches was uncovered?"

Brannigan's confidence slipped a little. He hadn't noticed. His inspection had been cursory. "It didn't seem dangerous to me at the time."

"So you did notice it — and took no steps to have it covered."

Brannigan was silent.

"You'll agree, Mr. Brannigan, that it was dangerous. Had it been covered David Fleming would be alive now."

Lessing without any formal request to speak rushed in with, "Not necessarily. The accident could have occurred anywhere — off the harbour edge, off a gangplank. It could equally have occurred crossing the road. You can't wall boys up behind plate glass. All living is dangerous. The school has always taken every possible care of the boys. Its degree of contractual care has always been of the highest."

The coroner stopped him. "We're trying to determine why the child died in that particular way." He spoke to Thirza. "We know through hindsight that the uncovered hatch was dangerous. Do you want Mr. Brannigan to answer you, or was your question rhetorical?"

Thirza said crisply, "I'm sorry if I was pointing out the obvious. There was danger. A child died."

"Have you any other question for this witness?"

"No, sir."

Brannigan stepped down and Hammond took the stand. Brannigan under pressure had become a headmaster with an anaesthetised conscience. Now that the pressure was relaxed he felt the blood rushing in. He couldn't assess the degree of his own responsibility. Now, at this moment, it seemed total. The words *a child died* thrummed through his mind like an unsteady pulse beat.

Hammond under pressure was a great deal less than calm. His hands on the witness box were clenched fists of controlled aggression.

The coroner handled him carefully. "The main function of an enquiry of this kind isn't to apportion blame but to establish facts. Tell us in your own words what happened from the time you boarded the *Mariana* until you became aware of the child's fall."

The hot afternoon sun shining through the green curtains highlighted the sheen of sweat on Hammond's forehead. He looked around the courtroom and saw Fleming. He spoke his evidence, looking at him.

"I boarded the ship with eight boys. The three young ones stayed with me all the time, they were never out of my sight. The five older ones — including David Fleming — were given jobs to do in different parts of the freighter. It was understood that they would stay at their posts and get on with the job. The ship wasn't a playground. My discipline isn't lax. David Fleming was to have stayed on the poop deck and sketched the rudder machinery. It seemed to me reasonable that he should stay there without my mounting a guard over him. My eight-year-olds might conceivably have fooled around the hatch and fallen in. I credited a twelve-year-old with more sense."

Fleming half rose in anger and then sat again as the coroner quickly interposed. "Just stay with the facts, Mr. Hammond and I'd be obliged if you'd look at me as you speak."

"I beg your pardon."

"Carry on."

"During the hour or so before the accident I took the three younger boys to the bridge and supervised them while they did some sketching there. During this period I took them to the engine-room. Stonley, one of the older boys, was there and I wanted to see how he was getting on with his work on the engines. His was the most complicated task and I felt he needed the help. I then returned to the upper deck with the three young lads. They wanted to see inside one of the lifeboats and I had just lifted them in when . . ." he looked across at Fleming again and some of the brusqueness left his voice, "I heard David scream." His armpits were suddenly sour with sweat and he moved uncomfortably. "I didn't know what had happened — or how serious it was. I couldn't leave the three young boys in the lifeboat, so I had to get them out before investigating . . ." He looked towards the window. "It's damnably airless in here."

The coroner let his sympathy show ."It was a shocking experience. I know how painful it is for you to have to go over it again. Are you feeling unwell?"

"No, I'm perfectly well. It's just a very hot June day and those curtains don't do much to keep the sun out."

The coroner nodded to one of the police officers who went and opened the slats. If fresh air came in, it wasn't perceptible.

Fleming thought savagely, Bring on the sal-volatile — bring him a recliner — cosset him — tell him how good and reliable he is — wrap his bleeding conscience in bandages and send him home.

He felt a heavy sense of defeat. Hammond, on the face of it, was blameless.

The coroner prompted him. "You heard the boy cry out. You got the three small boys out of the lifeboat. And then . . . ?"

"Another of the older boys — Masters — was in the captain's cabin which was nearby. I told Masters to keep an eye on the young ones while I went to investigate. Masters, himself, hadn't heard anything. The only lad who had heard the cry was Durrant. He was in the open air, on the fo'c'sle deck. He arrived at the hatch fractionally before I did."

"What was the time lapse between the shout and your arrival on the scene?"

"A matter of minutes — three — four — perhaps five."

The coroner addressed Thirza. "The evidence about the drawing was largely conjectural. At this stage of the inquest we're dealing with facts. As Mr. Fleming's legal representative I don't want you to feel you're being restricted in any way. If you want to confer with Mr. Fleming on any point — then please do."

"Thank you, sir, but Mr. Fleming and I had a full discussion before coming to court."

"Have you a question to ask this witness?"

"Please. Mr. Hammond, wouldn't you say five minutes was an unreasonably long time before you went to investigate?"

Hammond's adrenalin flowed even faster in the face of a new enemy. A good-looking, suave, elegant little bitch. "I didn't time myself with a stop-watch, it could have been less."

"When you heard the child cry out, how did you know which child screamed?"

"There was only one child in the region of the poop deck."

"Where the open hatch was?"

"Near where the open hatch was."

"When you arrived did you go directly to the poop deck or did you look down the hatch into the hold?"

"I looked down the hatch into the hold."

"You thought it probable that David had fallen down it?"

Hammond, aware of gin traps under soft undergrowth, trod warily. "Durrant — the older boy — was already there. He indicated that David had fallen."

"Indicated? Could you tell me more clearly what you mean? Did he say 'David has fallen down the hold' or 'I saw David falling down the hold' . . . .?"

"I don't remember. I can't see that it matters what he said — or didn't say."

"There is rudder machinery on the poop deck. David was supposed to be there on an assignment. The accident could have happened there. You could have been expected to go there directly. The hold itself is fairly dark. If you went directly to the hold expecting to see the child there then you must have had a reason. If the boy, Durrant, told you to look there, then that is a reason. If he didn't, then you must have anticipated the accident. You must have been aware of the danger of the uncovered hatch. If you were and did nothing about it then you failed in your contractual duty of care."

Lessing was on his feet. "I don't like your imputations."

The coroner, who didn't like them either, liked Lessing's interruption even less. He told him to sit again. "Answer Miss Crayshaw's question, Mr. Hammond. Were you aware of the danger of the open hatch?"

"No, sir. If I had been I wouldn't have set the lad's assignment so near it."

"You wouldn't have gone directly to it if young Durrant hadn't made it plain to you that the child had fallen there?"

"No."

"And you can't remember Durrant's words?"

"No."

"That's understandable. When you realised the child had fallen down the hatch into the hold, what did you do?"

Hammond felt the salt of sweat on his lips. It was caking at the corner of his mouth. He didn't want to remember the hold — or the climb down into it. He tried to disassociate the mental image from the words, but with no success. The words came out painfully.

"He was lying on his face. I had never seen anyone with a broken neck. I didn't touch him. I could see he was dead. I climbed out of the hold. I thought I was going to vomit. I went to the rail."

The coroner's voice was toneless. "You noticed that his eyes were bandaged?"

"Yes."

"His hands were free?"

"Yes."

"You didn't touch him at all?"

"No."

"What happened then?"

"Mr. Sherborne came over from the ship that was anchored close by. The doctor and police were sent for."

"And we have their evidence. Mr. Hammond, have you any ideas on how the child came to fall?"

"No."

"He was in your House at school?"

"Yes."

"So you knew him quite well?"

"As well as one can know any child."

"It has been suggested — again we're back in the realms of conjecture — that he might have been acting out a game, a pirate game perhaps, anyway some sort of fantasy that involved a blindfold. Does that sort of thing equate with what you knew of the child?"

"It's possible. He enjoyed acting. It could have happened that way."

The coroner addressed Lessing. "And now, Mr. Lessing, have you anything to ask?" The rebuke was implicit.

Lessing bounced up from under it. "Yes. Mr. Hammond, has any child in your care ever had an accident before?"

"No."

"You are a conscientious man and you have an excellent reputation both up in the school and here in the town where we have a close liaison with the school. I believe that the standard of care shown was first-class. You couldn't have done more." He looked at Thirza. "Some of Miss Crayshaw's questions were difficult and distressing but you answered them honestly. The one other question I want to put to you is a very simple one — is your conscience clear on this matter?"

"Yes."

"Then that," said Lessing, "is good enough for me."

And nicely put, the coroner thought, if the jury needed convincing — which it didn't. The verdict of accidental death was already a foregone conclusion. Even so, justice needed to be seen to be done. The boy's father was sitting there as if he were witnessing a crooked dice game and was powerless to do anything about it. If he didn't feel he had to do everything possible to give him a fair deal he wouldn't call the last witness. He didn't like calling on juveniles to give evidence, but Durrant had been the first on the scene. It was Durrant who had indicated (blast Miss Crayshaw's insistence on the interpretation of this) to Hammond where the boy had fallen.

He thanked Hammond for his evidence and told him he could stand down.

Durrant took the stand.

Today he looked a man and was in his glory. The machine in his mind was functioning at high pitch and was fully controlled. He saw the courtroom as a room full of sub-normal aliens from an inferior satellite — a pusillanimous, cretinous bunch of observers. The only one there of any account was Fleming himself. He dared to look at him and then dared to smile at him. The smile, he saw with satisfaction, needled him like a poisoned dart.

He wondered if he should ask to affirm rather than to speak the oath and then decided against it. Shulter was sitting midway down the left aisle and if he affirmed now there would be long heart-searching sessions with him later. He had dropped God together with his mother yesterday — not that God had ever figured very much.

He read out the oath and then turned his attention to the coroner.

Breddon who had not looked forward to questioning a nervous and probably sensitive fifteen-year-old was put a little off-balance by what he saw. The lad was tall for his age and he was standing very straight with his shoulders back, almost a military stance. Brannigan hadn't described him this way. Brannigan's description had been sympathetic — something about a miserable home background, lack of confidence and so on. This boy, now, was almost scornful in his attitude as if he dealt with a bunch of fools.

All the same, he was a child. Breddon corrected himself — a child up to fourteen, a young person from fourteen to seventeen. He was a young person of relatively tender years and must be treated as such. He had already decided to use his christian name, but found it didn't come easily to him.

"I'm sorry you had to be called today, Steven, but you realise how important this enquiry is?"

Durrant looked at him with a degree of contempt. "Yes, sir."

"Did you know young David Fleming well?"

"No, sir."

"But he was in your House at school?"

"Yes, sir."

"Feel free to expand your answers, Steven. What we're

trying to do at this inquest is to understand the circumstances of David's fall."

"Yes, sir."

"You say you didn't know him well — would that be because of the age difference between you?"

"Yes, sir."

"I should have thought in the environment of a boarding school, with its separate Houses, there would have been a family atmosphere."

"No, sir."

Breddon, suspicious that the monosyllabic answers were deliberately insolent, said sharply, "Why not?"

Durrant had a quick mental image of his mother in bed with the photographer. Why was this man going on about families?

"A school is a school, sir."

"Meaning?"

"There is no family atmosphere."

Breddon had to accept it. "I see." He abandoned his atttempt to get to know David through the eyes of another boy. "You were called to give evidence, Steven, because you were the first on the scene of the accident."

"Yes, sir."

"Tell us about it."

Durrant, forced into speech of more than one sentence, took his time in answering. He glanced casually at Brannigan, hardly seeing him, and then looked at David's father again. The power-house in his mind felt a sudden surge that ramified through his whole nervous system. As Hammond had earlier, he spoke to Fleming alone.

"I was sketching in the fo'c'sle when I heard a scream. It came from the other end of the ship — the poop deck. I went to see what had happened. I looked down the hatch and saw David lying in the hold. He was dead." He lingered on the word dead. It came out gently.

Breddon, equally gently, asked, "Why did you look down the hold?"

"I could see there was no-one on the poop deck. I had to pass the hatch to get to the poop deck. It was the obvious place to look."

"You didn't see him fall?"

"No, sir."

"You have heard since that he was blindfolded?"

"Yes, sir."

"Have you any thoughts on that?"

"Kids do corny things, sir. He was only twelve."

Fleming felt the words — only twelve — like a deliberate bruising. The mockery in Durrant's eyes had come and gone. He was looking away from his now and back at the coroner.

Breddon, not insensitive, had been aware of the nuance, but didn't know how to interpret it. The sooner he got the boy off the stand the better. "Mr. Lessing, have you any question to ask this witness?"

"No. I think the boy gave his evidence very well."

"Miss Crayshaw?"

Thirza shook her head. She felt she walked a foggy landscape on a dark night. The boy gave her the creeps, but she couldn't fault him.

The coroner told him to stand down.

He made his speech to the jury as brief as possible. "We don't know why David Fleming fell. Had his hands been tied his death might have had more sinister overtones. Fortunately they were not. He applied the blindfold for a reason we'll never know. It's possible he was playing a game of some kind. The sketch you have been shown might indicate a disturbed state of mind, but we have had no expert witness to confirm this. You must consider the possibility of suicide, but there is no solid evidence to support it. The boy came to Marristone Grange almost a year ago, following the death of his mother. There is no reason to suppose that he didn't settle happily into the life of the school. The reputation of the school is high in the town. You might believe that the *Mariana* was hazardous — indeed, it turned out to be — but the care taken of the children seems to me to be reasonable. The poop deck was a safe area, if the child had stayed there all would have been well. I shall ask you to retire now, give the matter careful thought, and then return with your verdict."

The jury took less than five minutes.

All seven tradesmen and true were unanimous. The school would continue to be painted and plumbed and cleaned and fed. There wasn't a stain on its character.

The foreman, who was also the local butcher, spoke the verdict. "Accidental death . . . and may we express sympathy with the boy's father?"

Fleming was already on his feet and on his way out of the court. For the first time that afternoon he saw David — the features, the wing of his eyebrows, the steady look from the hazel eyes.

He felt a terrible sense of failure.

The inquest had been a charade.

"You're dead," he told David in his mind. "My arms are around your shoulders, you're standing out here in the sunshine with me — and there isn't any bloody justice anywhere."

Jenny had followed him out. She was about to put her hand on his, but she let it drop. He wasn't aware of her or of anyone. His isolation was complete. He saw no-one but his son.

Ten

"A BOTTLE OF the best bubbly," Lessing said. I bought it on my way to the court as a gesture of confidence." He put it down on Alison's Georgian table, pushing aside her display of antique paperweights.

She was blooming again, he noticed, like a half-dead flower plunged into fresh water. The verdict had been tonic enough without the champagne. The champagne was a bonus.

Brannigan, he knew, would deem it indecent to celebrate too openly. Here, up at the school house, within an hour of the verdict, they could be as indecent as they chose.

Alison, smiling, went to fetch the glasses.

Brannigan would have preferred Scotch, but drank the champagne to please her. On the drive back to the school she had lavished him with praise. He had given his evidence perfectly. He couldn't have done better. He was the rock on which the school stood. Saint Peter, he had told her dryly, had had his moment of denial, too — in fact three of them — he wondered if he had felt three times as bad.

She had looked at him, quite patently at a loss. "What do you mean?"

It seemed unkind to turn off the glow. "Nothing. The verdict was fair, I suppose."

"You suppose? You should be jumping over the moon. Today the school had justice done to it. It's a good school and you know it — the whole town knows it. No harm has been done."

He refrained from stating the obvious. He had seen Fleming's expression as he had stood outside the court. Even

Jenny had got nowhere with him. He had walked off through the crowd as if he walked a desert.

Lessing drank two glasses of champagne before taking his leave. He wondered if he would see the Crayshaw woman again. Fleming's bird had beautiful plumage. She had fluttered at the inquest without much effect. Had she flown in less alien country she might have achieved a different verdict — but he doubted it. Her inside knowledge was nil. His own suspicions were another matter, but they would keep for another day. Let Alison have her moment of glory. Later, some neat and discreet patchwork over the cracks should restore the fabric of the school. Today's verdict had given the old *alma mater* a future. He had noticed two of the governors at the inquest — Colonel Goldthorpe and Mrs. Telford. Afterwards they had gone to have a word with the coroner. No graft, of course. Breddon couldn't be bought. They were buddies up at the links. Mrs. Telford was lady captain this year and Mrs. Breddon was vice-captain. It didn't signify anything, but it all helped. If the school had crashed there would have been one hell of a financial loss.

Alison walked to the door with him and waved him off the premises. Normally she didn't like him. Today she did. When she returned to the sitting room she saw that Malcolm had gone to sit with his back to the open window. There was a small breeze now though the day was still very sultry. It ruffled through his thinning hair and she went over and smoothed it. "You're sitting in a draught. You'll get a chill."

It was the first time she had touched him in days and he smiled at her with a degree of affection. The wine had taken the edge off his disquiet and allowed optimism to creep through. He was glad he had done what he did — not only for her sake but for the sake of the whole school. There was the sound of boys' voices in the air. Cricket on a summer's day. The academic results hadn't been bad this year, considering the smallness of the sixth form. There had been some

Oxbridge successes. Next year the potential was even better. He liked teaching. If he could get more help on the administrative side he might be able to have more time in the classroom. He needed to adopt a more positive approach. As from now he would try to see things with fresh eyes. It didn't do to dwell on failure. He wished he could get Fleming's face out of his mind.

Corley senior arrived at the school at twenty minutes to five. He had intended arriving in time for the inquest, but a natural reticence had kept his foot from pressing too hard on the accelerator. Rage coupled with anxiety had made all things seem possible when he had set out on the journey, but as time had gone by he knew he couldn't do it. He hadn't been called as a witness. A dramatic denouement from the back of a crowded courtroom might be possible in the mind, but couldn't be done in fact. He knew nothing at all about courtroom procedure. He had never attended an inquest in his life. To make a statement out of turn might result in being charged with contempt of court. Neville, distressed and tearful, was safe. Dramatic gestures, desirable as they might be, were for the extroverts of this world, not for mild-mannered bank managers.

He paused in the town long enough to buy a packet of cigarettes and find out what the verdict had been. Not surprised by it, he drove straight up to the school. The games period was coming to an end now and the boys were strolling over to the main building. He stood and watched them for a moment, and then he went up the cracked steps to the door of the school house and rang the bell. His anger was cocooned inside him.

Alison, opening to him, saw a corpulent middle-aged man wearing a well-cut grey suit. She had met him once before, but he was one of the parents who rapidly became faceless in retrospect. His wife, loud, lean and enthusiastic, she would have remembered quite clearly, but this man she remembered not at all. She thought he might be the first of the reporters — they always took longer to arrive in time of good news — and she had a speech prepared. Her smile was welcoming. "Yes?"

He remembered her. "I should like a word with your husband, Mrs. Brannigan."

She knew Malcolm wouldn't handle the interview half as well as she would. The Press would sniff out his doubt and pounce on it. "He's rather busy at the moment — won't I do?"

"I hardly think so. You don't remember me, do you? I'm Neville Corley's father."

Her smile became tight and frozen before her lips closed. She stood aside and indicated that he should come in.

Brannigan, he noticed, wasn't busy at all. He was slumped in his chair looking half asleep. There was a bottle of champagne on the table.

He said quietly, "Celebrating?"

Brannigan got to his feet. Not poised as high as Alison, there was no euphoria to quench. A sudden pain of apprehension came and went. He held out his hand. "Mr. Corley, I'm glad you've come."

Corley ignored it. "May I sit down?"

"Please do."

Alison, her voice unnaturally high, asked how Neville was. He answered dryly, "Alive."

Brannigan, aware of animosity deliberately overt and not to be ignored, became tense. "The police told us he was safely home. We were extremely worried. I tried contacting you several times by phone."

"I left the receiver off. The lad had a great deal to tell me."

"You brought him back? Where is he now — out in the car?"

"No." Corley picked up an empty champagne glass, studied it and put it down. "Accidental death, wasn't it? A cause for celebration."

Brannigan didn't answer. Alison, who had been standing by the door, felt she could stand no longer. She went and sat on a small upright chair near the china cabinet. To sit at ease in this man's presence would be like trying to sit near a time-bomb. A foreboding of catastrophe filled her like a dark cloud.

Brannigan waited for what was to come.

Corley said, "It was the wrong verdict."

Brannigan asked him to explain.

Corley took his time about it, and the words were clipped with controlled anger. "My son and young David Fleming were friends. They were in different Houses, but they met in class. They both got keen on learning semaphore — it arose through the maritime project. By coincidence Neville's assignment was on the poop deck of the sister ship to the one that David was on. They were close enough to see each other. Instead of getting on with their task they played at signalling each other. Your resident psychopath — Durrant — left his post for some reason best known to himself. If young Fleming had needed to be punished for not getting on with the job then it wasn't up to a twisted adolescent to do it. He hauled the boy down to the deck where the open hatch was — he tied his hands and blindfolded him. It might have ended there but David goaded him with accusations about a homosexual relationship with Innis, the sportsmaster — nicknamed Bruin. 'Woolly Bear on Durrant's bed'. Durrant gave him a back-hander — and then another that took him over the edge of the hatch and into the hold. Durrant went down after him. When he came up again he was carrying the tie that had been around his wrists. Presumably he would have taken off the blindfold had there been time — there wasn't. The verdict today should have been murder."

Brannigan felt no surprise. He felt battered and ill, but not surprised. The possibility had been in his mind for days.

He said stiffly, " 'Woolly Bear on D's bed' — not Durrant's bed. Your lad got that bit wrong."

"D's — Durrant's — the implication's the same."

"It may seem so, but it isn't." It must have seemed so to Durrant, he thought, for him to have reacted so violently. "I find it difficult to believe that Innis . . ." It trailed off. Innis, nicknamed Bruin. Bruin — Woolly Bear. It all tied in.

Alison exploded out of her silence. "It's the most appalling lies. Jesus Christ — you're not going to sit there and take it!"

Brannigan and Corley looked at her and then at each other. Corley said stiffly, "There's more — not lies, very ugly truth, I'm afraid. Perhaps Mrs. Brannigan should leave us."

She answered for herself before Brannigan could. "No! You'll not get me out. Someone has to be here to . . ." She didn't finish it.

Brannigan finished it in his mind. ". . . defend the honour of the school". He had a momentary vision of her father declaiming in the Elysian fields on the sins of mortal flesh, prior to castrating Innis and kicking Durrant into the depths of hell.

Poor Alison, he thought. She looked stripped to the bone. He felt very sorry for her.

Corley went on. "My lad as witness to murder was next in line himself." He misinterpreted Brannigan's expression. "No, I'm not dramatising. I'm giving you facts. Durrant tried to get out of him how much he had seen. There was a session down in your copse interrupted by someone — a fat bloke with a plummy voice was how Neville described him. Neville had been sick after being almost suffocated when he ran into him."

Lessing, Brannigan thought.

"The night my son made off home, Durrant cornered him

in the locker room. His language was filthy — how much my son understood I wouldn't care to guess. There might have been violence if the locker room had been more remote. Durrant didn't touch him. He threatened him. The threats were enough. It took Neville a night and most of the next day to get home. He's got the beginnings of bronchitis, but he's tucked up in a safe bed. I don't know how scarred he is emotionally. When I told him that he must tell you exactly what he told me, that what I tell you is hearsay, he looked as if I had shown him a deaths-head. He's frightened out of his mind, but he'll tell you — and anyone else who needs to be told."

Brannigan rallied a little. It was hearsay. His instinct was to believe it, but nothing had been said that couldn't have been made up. And then he remembered the sketch again. David after drawing it had immediately given it to Jenny. Woolly Bear. Symptom of distress. Innis alias Bruin. Young Corley hadn't a devious mind. He wouldn't have made that up. Lessing had said that he was scared out of his wits.

Corley broke through his thoughts. "I came to you before going to the police. It's up to you now to report it to the police. I advise you to report it without delay."

"The lad is fifteen."

Corley shrugged. "He's a psychopath."

"Then he needs medical help."

"Which your local G.P. can't give him. The rest of the lads here are your responsibility. How many more lads are you planning to put at risk before you do something about it?"

Brannigan felt very old, very tired. He walked slowly over to the door. "You're right, of course. None. But he deserves a hearing. I'll see him in my study over in the main building. You'd better come along."

Alison made one last effort. "If what you say is true —

and I can't believe it is — then let Durrant be put away quietly. Send for his parents. Let them see to it. It isn't our affair."

"Oh, but it is," Brannigan said gently, "very much our affair." He added, "I'm sorry."

He didn't know what he was apologising for. For insisting on doing his duty now when it was too late. For running the school remotely and comfortably instead of being in the thick of it. For being kind to the incompetent. For not suspecting Innis. For being weak.

Durrant, summoned to the Headmaster's study, went with a quick and buoyant step. He was still jubilant after the inquest. His role had been more brief than he would have liked. There had been no real pitting of wits. The coroner, as spineless as a jellyfish, had oozed concern over the proceedings. The only rock had been Fleming himself and he hadn't uttered. To pit his wits against Fleming would have been a joy.

"Yes, Headmaster?"

He noticed Corley sitting over in the leather chair — the same chair that he had sat in himself when he had spoken to his mother on the telephone. The association caused a blending of shock and remembered pain. He winced.

Brannigan noticed. "Come in, Durrant, and close the door behind you." He wondered how Durrant had recognised Corley. He went on to make the introductions as if he hadn't noticed. "This is Mr. Corley — Neville's father."

"I know."

"How do you know?"

"They were together on sports day."

And neither of your parents were there, Brannigan thought. At all school functions you roamed alone. It was all very well to try to stamp out pity when the lad wasn't there. He was there now. Not the Durrant of the courtroom

160

brazening it like a Nazi recruit, but the gangling awkward boy shrugging off his height, trying to diminish himself into obscurity.

"Do you know why Mr. Corley is here?"

"Yes." In lucid moments he had known that this meeting now was inevitable. Ever since Neville Corley had gone he knew that there could be only one outcome. When his mind played the games he wanted it to play anxiety was programmed out. Corley wouldn't arrive home. He would arrive home and say nothing.

Now, briefly lucid, he accepted the situation for what it was.

Brannigan said with a degree of gentleness, "Tell us." He stood up and pulled out a chair. "Don't be frightened — just tell us."

The gentleness was puzzling. Durrant declined to sit. He held the back of the chair. If you tried to trap a tiger you laid a bait of meat, you didn't make pussy-cat noises at it. What did the old fool think he was — a backyard moggie? Now that the shock was receding, he was beginning to feel better again. He examined Corley senior with some intentness. He hadn't done anything about the warts on the back of his left hand. On sports day he had been showing his son how to hold the bat and the warts had been obvious. Innis couldn't have liked that very much. Showing the boy how to hold the bat was his business. Innis. Bruin. He had never called him Bruin to his face. Last night it had been Sir. The conversation dribbled back into his mind. 'Durrant, you're a sadistic brute — what the hell were you trying to do to that poor little brat?' 'Nothing.' 'Nothing, *sir* . . . You're sick, Durrant, do you know that?' 'Then make me well sir, you know how, sir, there's time, sir, before the bell, sir,' . . . 'Get out!'

He turned back to Brannigan. "David Fleming walked in his sleep."

"And so —?"

"He woke up twice — by my bedroom."

"Go on."

"He saw Bruin. Bruin didn't see him. I didn't tell Bruin."

"Bruin — Mr. Innis?"

"Yes. I thought Fleming was still asleep when he walked into my room. He walked in very quietly and he walked out very quietly. On the *Mariana* he called Bruin Woolly Bear. On D's bed. My bed. I killed him."

A perfectly good reason, Durrant thought. He looked at the two men and wondered why they should look at him as they did. He had never intended shopping Innis. Innis had been his sole comfort for a long time. Last night, after leaving Innis, he had gone down to the hollow at the bottom of the copse and lain on his stomach and cried. The tears had been shed for his mother, too. It was hard to cut adrift from people. At the inquest he had felt liberated. He had stood alone and been powerful. He didn't feel powerful now. A great longing for Innis surged over him. The rejection last night had seemed final. It couldn't be final. Not his mother and Innis in one day. There was a metallic thumping in his skull. He pressed his fingers against his temples trying to stop it. The engine was running again but running too fast.

He said very politely, "Excuse me, Headmaster. I think I'm going to be sick."

He left the room before they could stop him and ran across the main hall. The quickest way to the gym was through the kitchen garden. He vaulted rows of cabbages and left a trail of leaves. With a sudden burst of amusement he kicked at an upstanding onion and sent it spinning across the soil. The awful school food. The awful school garden. The awful school. He was half-laughing, half-crying, when he reached the gym. Six little boys were lined up to vault the wooden horse. Innis, hairy in shorts and sweat shirt, was leaning against the wall bars watching them.

Durrant said, "It's over. You're for the chop." He couldn't look at Innis as he said it.

A little boy with tight ginger curls was shaping up for the jump. Durrant took him by his hair and the seat of his pants. "Whoops — up and over!" The boy screamed in protest as Durrant flung him over and on to the mat. He fell heavily, sobbing.

Innis went to help him. He stood him up and got him to walk and then he turned to the others. "Out — all of you — out." His face was grey.

The children, frightened like sheep with a wolf amongst them, herded together in a frozen mass.

Innis headed the child who had fallen in the direction of the door. "Line up behind Sibley. Quick — one, two — one, two. March back to the changing room and stay there. Now!"

The line straggled out of the gym and then once through the door broke up. They ran in silence.

Durrant, breathing fast, was leaning against the horse. "I didn't mean to shop you. You could always say it wasn't true."

"What wasn't true?" Innis's pallor was stabbed with brown freckles.

"That you and I . . ."

"That you and I — what?"

"David Fleming knew about us — he saw us — that's why I killed him. I killed him for you."

The supreme gesture, he thought, what more could I do for you? He taunted you — Woolly Bear — and I closed his sodding mouth for ever. Be kind to me, Bruin. Be pleased.

He wondered why Innis was taking such a long time to answer.

Innis spoke at last — very softly. "You stupid little bastard. You goddamned stupid little bastard. You're off

163

your bloody head." There was a sour taste on his tongue and the words were forced out of him sour with shock. The boy was mad. He had guessed for some time that he was unbalanced. And he, himself, had been mad to let things get as far as they had. He had started by feeling sorry for him. There had been something doglike about Durrant in the early days of the relationship. A pat. A word of praise. Or, rather, a reversal of the sequence. A word of praise. A pat. A caress. And then all of it. He wondered how much Brannigan would believe. The word of a boy gone crazy as opposed to his?

Durrant said in a very normal voice, "I love you."

"Crap!"

"Please . . ." Durrant took a couple of steps towards him.

"Get the hell away from me." He put his hand out to stop Durrant getting any closer. His fingers touched Durrant's forehead and he withdrew them as if the contact had made him unclean.

The gesture was as final and as wounding as it could be.

Durrant said, "All right. I'll get the hell away from you. As far as anyone can get away from anyone." His stomach felt like a coil of scorpions and his extremities were leaden. He doubted if he could move.

There was sufficient rapport between them for Innis to be aware of the depth of his pain. He was past caring. The fact that Durrant had done murder was of less importance than the reason for it. Durrant could kill both his reputation and his career. That mattered. He said, "They'll put you away for years." It came out viciously.

"And you, Bruin Boy — you." Gobbets of blood, Durrant thought. We spit them at each other. There's nothing more.

He found he could walk now, his thighs were cold and heavy, but they could move.

Appalled, Innis watched him as he went over to the wall

bars under the east window and began climbing. Near the top rung he held on with one hand and leaned over to grab the climbing rope which was suspended from the ceiling. Carefully holding it, he climbed up on to the window-sill. Squatting there he made a noose with the rope and slipped it around his neck. His eyes were diamond bright and his face was flushed.

Innis thought, God — no! — but the words stayed in his mind.

Brannigan pushing open the swing doors behind him caught him a glancing blow on his shoulder, but was unaware of it. He shouted out the protest that Innis couldn't voice.

That Durrant would come for refuge to the gym hadn't taken much working out. He and Corley had come through the main building and they had come as fast as they could — but not fast enough. Corley, at his side, spoke quietly. "Easy, and gently, don't raise your voice."

Brannigan, about to rush across to the bars, stopped just inside the room. "Durrant — Neville —" He realised that in his panic he had the wrong christian name. "Steven . . ."

Durrant laughed. "You're not very good at it, are you?"

The laughter, high and sweet and insane, sent an icy sweat down Brannigan's spine. "At what?"

"At being human."

"What do you mean, Steven?" Calm him, he thought. Make him talk. If there's to be an impulse jump, it will happen now.

"That's right — you've got it right, this time. What's Lambert's name?"

"Which Lambert?" All the boys' names had gone out of his mind. He wasn't even aware he had a Lambert.

"There's only one. In Sherborne's House. Mr. Innis remembers it — don't you Mr. Innis?"

Innis found it difficult to speak at all. He got it out eventually. "Michael."

"That's right. Mr. Innis is human. Sometimes. He used to use my christian name, too, sometimes. He doesn't use it any more."

Brannigan said, "He will if you want him to." He took a couple of steps across the room and Durrant immediately hunched up on the window sill, his neck thrust forward. "I'll jump if you come any nearer."

Brannigan stood still. "I'll do anything you want me to. And nothing you don't want me to. Just take that rope off your neck and come down."

Durrant said conversationally, "It's Rampton, isn't it?"

"What is?"

"The place where they send criminal lunatics." He looked at Innis. "Those who are off their bloody heads."

Brannigan soothed, "You're a sick child. If you'll come down nothing awful will happen to you. You'll be taken to a hospital and made well."

"Pussy-cat noises."

"What?"

"Try meat?"

"What?"

"You're either deaf or incredibly stupid."

Brannigan said humbly, "Just tell me what to do."

Durrant thought, I've got you. While I sit here with this rope around my neck, I've got you. The old power-machine in his mind, after one or two initial lurches in the wrong direction, was humming away beautifully. Power, like strong drink, was a river in his veins.

"Take your jacket off."

"My jacket?"

"You heard me."

Brannigan unbuttoned his grey jacket, got out of it, and held it in his left hand.

"Put it on the floor."

Brannigan let it drop.

"Now stand on it."

Brannigan stood on it."

"You wear braces."

"Yes."

"That's very old-fashioned of you. Bruin wears a belt."

"Bruin is — with it."

"Don't try bridging the generation gap, old man. Use your own vocabulary."

"I'm sorry."

"Don't be sorry. Be your age. You're past it, you know. You should have retired long ago."

Brannigan whispered a heart-felt amen to that. He half-turned his head and saw that Corley had gone — presumably to raise the alarm. He hoped he would raise it with caution. Innis was still there.

"Now take your trousers off."

Brannigan hesitated. Durrant fingered the rope around his neck and moved nearer the edge of the sill.

Brannigan removed his trousers. The June day was still very hot, but he stood and shivered in his underpants and vest. He hoped Durrant wouldn't make him strip to the nude.

Durrant looked at him critically. "As I said — old. Drop your trousers on top of your jacket and stand on them."

Brannigan did so.

"Now sing to me."

"Sing what to you?"

"No, don't sing what to me — just sing. Sing the school song."

Brannigan racked his brains. The school song? They hadn't a school song. In Assembly they sang whichever hymns Laxby chose from the hymn book. He tried humming a few bars from the Doxology.

Durrant began to laugh. "You are a fool — an almighty fool." This time his laughter was normal.

Brannigan felt his anger rise. The boy was having him on. He wasn't off his head. He was sadistically sane. "Now look here . . ." He moved forward.

Durrant's face contorted. His voice came out as a roar. "Stand still!"

Brannigan stood.

"That's better. You don't want to kill me, do you?" It was plaintive.

"I'm asking you to come down."

"Ask away, sonny, ask away. Do you know my mother's a whore?"

Brannigan didn't know how to answer that one. It seemed polite to deny it — so he did so.

"And my father's an idiot."

He said no to that, too.

"Don't keep contradicting me. I know them. You don't. Give me one good reason for going on living."

Brannigan thought for a couple of minutes. "Your individuality. You are you — not your parents."

"What's so good about being me?"

"There's good in everyone."

"What's my special good?"

It seemed a brainwave. "Your capacity to love."

Durrant began to cry. He cried open-eyed and silently.

Brannigan said gently, "Steven . . ."

"The one good reason not to live." It came out raggedly. He fingered the rope again.

"Steven . . ."

"And don't Steven me — the name's Durrant. You're soft. You're all soft here." He said after a silence of several minutes, "I'm bored with you. I'm bored with all of you. Fetch Fleming."

"Fleming?"

"F-l-e-m-i-n-g. David's father. I want him."

The words were out before Brannigan could stop them. "But you killed his son."

"That's right," Durrant said laconically. "Let Bruin fetch him — and you stay here. Tell him he's got to come."

Eleven

FLEMING WAS LYING on his bed, empty-minded, watching the sunlight shimmering on the ceiling. Thirza, aware that he lay in a limbo she couldn't enter, had packed and gone. She had slipped a note under his door — an apology for a non-brilliant performance at the inquest and a request that he should phone her the next day. He saw the note lying there and hadn't bothered to open it. His mind refused to tick over at all. Anger and disappointment and grief had lain on him like scum on still water. Tiredness had distilled it all into a state of almost-peace.

The knock on his bedroom door was something to be ignored. He watched the lifting of the pale curtains in the breeze, the movement fragmented the sunshine into petals of light.

Jenny said, "Open to me, please."

His first reaction was resentment. The steel bars around David and himself were capable of being moved by one person only. If she forced her way through, he would think again and feel again. He wasn't ready for her. Not yet.

"John — I must see you."

"Damn you, Jenny — go away." He didn't know if he said it or thought it.

"Please."

Pain was flowing back. He got off the bed and went and unlocked the door. The sunlight from his bedroom spilled out on to the dark landing and washed over her so that her hair blazed. Her vitality as opposed to David dead was almost an offence.

She walked past him into the room.

She hadn't wanted to come. In normal circumstances she wouldn't have come. For days now he had seen the inquest as a kind of peak in his quest for retribution and it had turned out to be nothing of the kind. This new peak that she was to show him was so horrifying that she didn't know how to begin.

She noticed the envelope on the floor and handed it to him. "I know you want to be on your own."

He opened it and read the note. "An apology from Thirza. Not necessary. She did what she could."

It was an opening, but she couldn't take it.

He crumpled the note and put it on the dressing-table.

They looked at each other in silence. And then they walked towards each other and he was holding her. He could feel the warmth of her body through the light cotton of her dress and the hardening of her nipples under his hand.

She forced him away from her. "I didn't come to sleep with you."

The vehemence of her withdrawal puzzled him. He hadn't wanted her, but now he did. The periods of isolation would come and go. They were necessary. But at the end of them she had to be there. Grief, he thought, was a selfish indulgence. He began thinking about her.

She looked tense, almost furtive.

"What's the matter?" The concern in his voice held a degree of gentleness.

Still she couldn't say it. She went and sat on the edge of the bed.

"Jenny?"

An ambassadress of the school. Brannigan's words of several days ago came back to her. Brannigan, of an hour ago, still under Durrant's eye, had been rather more terse. "He wants Fleming. Get him. He'll come for you."

She had been too shocked to argue, or to think.

She picked up a handful of quilt and began pleating it. He came and sat beside her on the bed and took the quilt out of her hand. He asked it again, "What's the matter?"

And then it came out, roughly, baldly. At the end of it she said, "Durrant's threatening to kill himself. He's climbed on to a window-sill in the gym. He's tied a rope around his neck. He says he's going to jump. He wants you there."

The words were like so many blows to the head. Fleming felt himself reeling under them. He got up from the bed and went over to the washbasin. He filled a tumbler with water, but couldn't hold it steady. The water splashed over his wrists. He drank a little and then poured the rest away.

Jenny's voice as if from a distance went on in clear precise hammer-strokes. "He's out of his mind. Corley's father used the word psychopath. The police are up at the school. Shulter's there, too. He tried talking to Durrant, but he's worse than useless. Dr. Preston's been sent for, but I don't know what good he can do. Durrant's parents can't be located. I doubt if Durrant wants them anyway. He keeps shouting for you."

She looked at his back, wondering if he would ever answer. He had been standing at the basin, head bowed, for several minutes.

She said into the silence. "Durrant could jump on impulse at any time. I think you could stop him."

171

Fleming spoke at last. His voice burned with intense hatred. "Why should I stop him?"

"Because he's fifteen."

"David was twelve."

"He's sick. Not responsible."

"Sick — maybe. David's dead."

She had seen the mission at the outset as useless, but she couldn't just get up and go. A reluctant compassion for Durrant held her there.

"The death of two children won't bring one child back."

"Don't call him a child. He wasn't a child at the inquest. God damn him — he looked at me and smiled!"

She remembered her conversation with Hammond when she, too, had refused to call him a child. "He's sick. Even in the bad old days of hanging he'd be put away for treatment."

He rounded on her, high patches of colour in his cheeks. "Are you asking me to care about him?"

"I'm asking you to come back with me to the school."

"So that I can witness him jump?"

"Retribution. That should please you. David's dead. Now go and be the executioner."

He winced. She noticed and the flame of anger went. "He sets some store by your being there. If you have that sort of influence over his mind, you can stop him."

"Or trigger him."

"There's that risk."

"Risk — or promise."

"You can't mean that."

"Oh, but I can and I do." He wanted to be alone again with his thoughts. She was demanding action in a new crisis and all he could feel was shock and hate.

"Go away, Jenny. Stop talking at me. Go down to the car and wait. If I don't join you in half an hour go back to the school on your own, I won't be coming."

She felt a small surge of hope, but was wise enough not to show it. She left him without another word.

After she had gone he went to his briefcase and took out David's folder, as if contact with it would clarify what he had to do. If he didn't go up to the school Durrant might jump — or he might not. Either way, his non-arrival there would be an opting out. Why was Durrant passing the buck to him? Why couldn't he bloody well get on with it. He had killed David and now he wanted to kill himself. All right. Let justice be done.

Fifteen.

Bloody fifteen.

What's so extenuating about fifteen? The child mind becomes an adolescent mind and then a man's mind. There are no deep lines of demarcation.

He opened the folder at a page of flags. They had been done in coloured inks. David had gone to a lot of trouble with them. He hadn't been bad at sketching. One unfinished flag with a triangle still to be coloured had the look of a gallows about it.

Jenny's words, sharp, contemptuous: Go and be the executioner.

He closed the folder and put it back in the briefcase.

It would be easy to pack his bags and go back to London. He could ditch Jenny and her demands. He could wash his conscience clear as snow and read about Durrant's death jump in the newspaper.

Why should Jenny care about Durrant and expect him to care about Durrant.

He wanted Durrant dead.

He examined the thought in cold and clear detail and couldn't deny it.

If he went up to the school the confrontation had to be positive — one way or the other.

Fifteen.

173

If not a child mind — then a sick mind?

According to Jenny. According to sweet, sane, demanding, accusing Jenny who knew damn all about it. Or about him. Had she no idea of the danger of the role she was thrusting on him? What did she expect him to do — play God with a godlike compassion? Didn't she understand what it felt like to bring up a child — to love a child — to lose a child?

Didn't she understand him at all?

There should be no confrontation with Durrant. He should opt out and keep the skin of his conscience intact.

But he couldn't.

The half-hour was almost up when he joined Jenny in the car. The expression in his eyes quenched her quick relieved smile when she saw him. His look promised her nothing other than that he would come.

They drove in silence through the June evening. Over the sea mackerel clouds tinged with pink and gold formed a fretwork against the clear pale blue of the sky. The air was sharp with salt and wood-smoke. The school building, yellow in the evening light, looked benign. All outdoor activities had been stopped and the boys were confined to the west wing. The deserted grounds, unnaturally quiet, looked like the gardens of a bygone age. A police car parked near the shrubbery gave the lie to the air of peace.

Detective Inspector Grant was the first to greet him. "It's good of you to come — especially under the circumstances." He went on to explain that though it was possible to enter the gymnasium window via a ladder on the outside wall and take Durrant by surprise, the risk was too great. "Any positive effort to get at him and he'll jump. He's not bluffing. We've managed to contact Dr. Preston and he'll be over soon wtih someone from Blenfield — the psychiatric hospital. In the meantime the lad keeps asking for you. Do what you can."

Shulter, arriving in time to hear this, took Fleming aside. He said bluntly, "If you're expecting a confession of guilt, sorrow and penitence — then go away again. I tried speaking reason to him. He's beyond reason. His mind is sick through mental aberration — yours is sick through bereavement. Don't go in there if you intend hazarding his life even more than it is now."

"I don't know what I intend."

"Then don't go in."

"I have to." He couldn't explain the compulsion. He looked from Jenny's strained white face to Shulter's troubled one. Now that she had him here she was standing back, unsure. If Durrant died, he'd lose her. It was something he sensed.

He had expected Brannigan to meet him in the corridor outside the gym, but met Hammond instead. Innis, warned to be on hand in case Durrant should call out for him, was waiting, sick with apprehension, in one of the changing rooms. He had no wish to see Fleming. His own guilt in the matter was like a carcinoma that had suddenly burst its confines and begun to spread.

Hammond's sense of guilt was considerably diminished. No-one could have foreseen this. The crust of his bellicosity had smoothed off into normal anxiety. He had even taken charge to some extent. It was his doing that the boys were kept well clear of the area. It was his persuasion that had sent a near-hysterical Alison Brannigan back to the school house with Mollie. He hoped Mollie would have the strength of character necessary to keep her there.

He indicated the closed double doors of the gym and spoke quietly. "The true verdict of the inquest is in there. Manslaughter due to insanity. I'm sorry for all that's gone before. I'm sorry for any part of it that's my fault."

Fleming thought, Murder — manslaughter — diminished responsibility — the virus was becoming more and more attenuated, in time it would become benign. He asked sharply where Brannigan was.

"In there. Under Durrant's eye. Durrant won't let him move."

Fleming pushed open the door and stood on the threshold.

Brannigan was sitting on the floor in the middle of the room. Surrounding him in a neat circle were carefully placed dumb-bells — relics of the early days of the school which were normally suspended along one of the walls. His thin arms were goose-pimpled and his shoulder blades, sharply prominent, were blue with cold. He sat as still as a guru deep in meditation. Durrant, legs crossed and leaning back against the glass of the window, was watching him intently. The old fool had pleaded for a rest. He was letting him rest. He was getting older by the minute. When he had put him through his paces with the dumb-bells his breath had got short and his face had turned mauve. Durrant had wondered who would die first and had fingered the rope speculatively. Not that he intended jumping until Fleming came.

And Fleming was here now.

Fleming who had tried to see some of it in his mind as a preparation wasn't prepared for what he saw.

Brannigan, aware of him, turned his head slightly.

Durrant said in a thin high voice, "Don't move. I haven't given you permission to move. You asked to rest. You'll rest."

Fleming went over to Brannigan. Brannigan's eyes beseeched him to have a care. Fleming, aware of nothing except a coldly growing anger, spoke crisply. "Get up."

I can't . . . he . . ."

"He won't jump. He has sent for me. We have things to discuss. If he jumps — he'll jump afterwards." He swung around to Durrant, "Right?"

The machine in Durrant's brain took a joyful leap into top gear. Here was the enemy. Here was his match.

"Right. But I give the orders around here."

"Not stuck up there with a rope around your neck you don't. Now, Headmaster — out!"

Brannigan got up on to his knees and then painfully to his feet. Every muscle in his body ached. He looked at his pile of clothes and then up at Durrant, hesitating.

Fleming picked them up for him. "Here. Now leave us."

He stepped back as he watched Brannigan walking over to the door and his foot caught one of the dumb-bells and sent it spinning. Brannigan was brought up sharply in his tracks as if he had been shot. He looked around fearfully.

Fleming said, "A dumb-bell — one of the magic circle. You placed them, I suppose?"

"Yes." Brannigan's eyes signalled a lot more.

Fleming ignored the signals. "Get someone to brew you up some coffee. You need a hot drink. And you can send in some for me —when I say so."

Brannigan nodded. The double doors clicked shut behind him.

"And now the old fool's gone," Durrant said, "you can pick up the dumb-bell and put it back with the others."

"I can," Fleming said. "There are many things I can do — just watch me." He picked up a dumb-bell and hurled it across the room so that it crashed against the store-room door. He picked up a second and sent it against the vaulting horse. A third smashed into the opposite wall bars and splintered. He paused, the fourth in his hand, and looked up at Durrant assessing his reaction. Some of the contained violence of the last few hours had been dissipated in noise. He sent the fourth dumb-bell up towards the ceiling where it connected with a light bulb and shattered it.

It was a release of aggression for him, too. A calculated risk. He would have liked to bombard Durrant with them and bring him down, but it was something he could only do in his mind and not in fact.

Fifteen — three years older than David.

He couldn't kill him.

He couldn't let him kill himself.

This was no time for self-analysis, but he was aware that he breathed more easily and that his heart-beat had steadied. Anger was replaced by calm. He took a chair from along the wall and put it roughly where Brannigan had been sitting. He took out a cigarette and lit it.

"Loud enough for you?"

Durrant fingered the rope. He had expected them to be thrown in his direction and was disappointed. Was this enemy weak too?

"You're as shitting yellow as the rest of them."

"How so?"

"You could have knocked me off."

Fleming inhaled and then exhaled slowly. "Easily. But I came here to talk. You can't hold a conversation with a corpse."

Durrant accepted it. Not weak. Biding his time.

He moved the rope until it was more comfortable.

"I killed David."

"I know."

"I knocked him down the hatch into the hold."

"Yes."

"Is that all you have to say — yes?"

"You're talking. I'm listening."

"That's all. I killed him."

Fleming felt a momentary loss of control and didn't speak for a moment or two. When he did the question came out levelly. "Why?"

Durrant's machine began running irregularly so that his thoughts began to escape like rabbits running down dark forest paths. He didn't know why. He couldn't remember why. Something to do with Innis and a photographer.

He said quite cheerfully, "I really don't know." He went

on, "Really this — really that. He's really rather 'refained.' His old man makes piss-pots." He looked at Fleming and began to laugh. "You don't make piss-pots. Christopher does. From Stoke."

Until then Fleming hadn't been sure what kind of mind he was dealing with. Now he was begining to know. Everything he had done so far had been instinctive. He sensed that the boy needed a will stronger than his own.

Durrant said, "I'll jump when you tell me to."

"Why do I have to tell you to?"

"Everything is ordered. We live in an ordered society. Didn't you know?"

"Nobody orders me. I do things my way."

"It's right that you should order me. I killed your son. You're my enemy."

"Why obey the order of your enemy?"

Durrant was silent. He said after a while, "I smoke."

"Are you asking for a cigarette?"

"Yes."

"Then take off the rope and come down and get one."

Durrant's eyes clouded with contempt. "Pussy-cat noises again."

Fleming shrugged. "I don't give a damn what you do. I'll throw them up to you if that's what you want."

"Then throw them."

"Take off the rope, put it somewhere handy by you. If you lean over to catch them you might slip."

"Accidental death."

"No — suicide too soon. You don't want that, do you?"

Durrant thought about it. He didn't want that. He would jump when he was ready — after he had had a cigarette.

He took off the rope and put it on the window-sill beside him. If Fleming or anyone else made a move he would have it back on in a couple of seconds.

Fleming considered possibilities and discarded them. The

time factor wasn't right. He threw up the packet of cigarettes. It bounced against the window pane and just missed Durrant's outstretched hand.

He said brusquely, "You'd be a bloody awful fielder on a cricket pitch."

"That's what Bruin says."

He threw them again and this time Durrant caught them.

"Who's Bruin?"

"Bruin. Woolly Bear. If David hadn't seen, I wouldn't have killed him."

Fleming asked carefully, "Hadn't seen who?"

"Bruin — in my room — that night." He looked down at the cigarette, his face clenched suddenly against tears.

Fleming said, "Matches coming up. Ready?"

"Yes."

He aimed carefully and they dropped on Durrant's right knee. Durrant's tears were under control. He lit the cigarette calmly.

"David," Fleming said, "used to have nightmares about a caterpillar. He called it Woolly Bear." The conversation was out of his depth now and he thought it unwise to pursue it. Durrant's emotional reaction hadn't been lost on him.

Durrant tried to make the connection and failed. Why the hell were they talking about caterpillars? He was up here in the control of a death machine and the enemy down there was beaming in on him. Very soon now the death machine would be aimed at the enemy. A kick at Fleming's throat as he fell. They would both go out together. He calculated the angle of the jump. Not easy to assess.

Fleming asked him when he had eaten last.

"I don't know. I can't remember."

"I'm about to have some coffee sent in. Do you want some?"

"No."

Fleming called over his shoulder. "Tell Brannigan to bring the coffee in now. One cup."

After a few minutes Brannigan, fully dressed again, pushed open the door and brought in one of the thick school mugs filled with strongly smelling coffee. Fleming took it without a word.

Brannigan tried palming a note. Fleming, aware that Durrant had seen, tore it up in simulated anger before Durrant could demand it. "Anything you have to say, you say loud and clear. Right?"

Durrant nodded approvingly.

"And whatever it is," Fleming went on, "it can wait . . . until Durrant and I are ready to hear it." This time to Durrant, "Agreed?"

"Yes."

Brannigan said weakly, "I'm sorry."

The note had said that Preston's car had broken down. He and the psychiatrist from Blenfield would come as soon as they could.

When they were alone again there was a period of silence during which Fleming drank the coffee and Durrant smoked. He didn't particularly want the cigarette. He was both hungry and thirsty.

"In any case," he said aloud, "it would be drugged."

Fleming read his mind. "No-one would drug me. And no-one would drug you sitting there. Personally I don't give a damn what happens to you — I've already said so — but those people outside there do."

"Those people out there? You're mad."

"Your parents, then?" Very dangerous ground.

"My mother's dead." He thought about the statement he had just made and decided it must be true. He didn't care very much.

Fleming said easily, "You're good at being on your own. So am I. I recognise your strength."

"Don't give me that sort of crap. You hate my guts."

"Of course. But I still recognise your strength . . . that's why I don't understand you."

"What don't you understand?"

"Why you should sit up there too bloody scared to come down. Are you afraid of the way I'd kill you?"

"You'd kill me?"

"Wouldn't you expect me to? You killed David."

Durrant drew on his cigarette and then stubbed it out. "How would you kill me?"

"I certainly wouldn't hang you — or applaud you if you hanged yourself — and I don't carry a gun." He put down the coffee cup and held out his hands. "That leaves these."

"That way?"

"There isn't any other."

Durrant considered it. A bird alighted on the window ledge outside. He watched it idly. It was small and brown. He moved and it was off in a flutter of wings and a burst of song. One for sorrow. Birds were the spirits of the dead. It was the dead David come to mock him.

He spaced out the words, "I — am — not — afraid — of — you."

"Then come down and prove it."

"It's a trick — the sort of trick those out there would use."

"Those out there haven't our own very personal relationship."

"Of hatred?"

"Of hatred."

"And," tentatively, "respect?"

"Yes."

He drew the rope nearer. "I don't know."

Fleming said, "It will take me three or four minutes to drink the rest of my coffee. You'll either come down then and face me. Or you won't have the courage and you'll stay where you are. I shan't be around to watch you jump.

You'll jump on your own. And my respect for you will end with you."

A lucid moment came. "And you expect me to buy that?"

"Please yourself. Find you own easy way out. It's up to you."

Durrant's head began to throb with indecision. He examined the noose and tightened it. If he placed the knot expertly it would be quick. If he didn't it would be slow and humiliating.

Fleming was drinking his coffee, not looking at him. He was sprawled indolently in his chair, long and lean and strong. Innis had been strong, too, strong and tender.

If the enemy meant what he said then that way out was the better way out. There had to be a way out. His misery was like maggots gnawing his flesh. He was sick of being alive. He looked at Fleming trying to bore into his mind.

Fleming looked up from his cup and held his gaze, steadily.

"Decided?"

"Yes."

Fleming put his cup on the floor. "Then — come."

Durrant looked over at the door and saw the shadows through the glass. "Bolt the door."

Fleming hesitated. The watchers outside would restrain him if restraint became necessary. The unlocked door had been a safety valve and now he had to operate without it.

Had to.

There was no option.

He went over to the door and dropped the inside bolt.

Brannigan, appalled, looked at the others in silence. Jenny, white-faced, avoided his gaze.

Hammond said flatly, "He'll kill him," and began pushing ineffectually at the door.

Durrant, cramped by his position, moved awkwardly on to the top rung and then looked over his shoulder down at Fleming. "Not until I reach the floor."

"No."

Fleming stood with arms folded watching him. The boy was climbing down the wall bars with slow ungainly movements. He looked like a spider on a web. Ugly. Fragile.

David in the sun. Small. Fair.

David in the hold of the ship. Unimaginable.

Durrant had reached the ground. He turned with his back to the bars and then took a step in Fleming's direction. He licked his lips, his eyes bright with anticipation. "Now."

And now I hand you over, Fleming thought. I don't touch you. I kick any remaining faith you have in anybody to hell. I con you, boy, because I don't bloody trust myself. He saw the expression on Durrant's face as he took a step back from him. This was betrayal of the worst kind. The final killing of confidence in a world outside himself. Durrant's fifteen years of experience became fifteen years of disillusionment. Whatever the appalling future held, this was the most appalling moment of all.

Durrant's lips were moving, but he wasn't getting any words out. His eyes were bright points of tears and hate as he stood there waiting. The ignominy of the moment would be a memory he would carry to the end of his days.

Fleming, his momentary weakness quenched, spoke brusquely. "I promised you. I keep my promises. And bloody well defend yourself."

Durrant, in a moment old, once more became young. Elation, tinged with fear, flooded him. He moved in, fists flying. Fleming, who could have finished him in a matter of seconds, gave him three minutes. He hit him hard, but with half his strength. He hit him for David, and he hit him for himself, but mainly he hit him for Durrant. This was

Durrant's truth. Durrant's faith in mankind — if his mind were ever cured enough to understand it.

Durrant, his nose bleeding and his cheek-bones bruised, felt the hard thud of Fleming's fist against his jaw. The gym began to revolve like a space capsule out of control as his knees gave way. He saw Hammond's face distantly through glass, and Brannigan's face. They were splintering the door in an effort to break it down.

And then, coming nearer and bending over him, Fleming's face.

This was it — the moment of death.

He waited for it.

Fleming said coolly. "You're good. In another few years when you're heavier and stronger you'll be better." He took out his handkerchief and wiped away some of the blood. He understood Durrant's unspoken question and answered it. "No . . . I might want to kill you, but I can't. You'll understand why when you're well."

He helped Durrant to sit against the wall. He looked repulsive and pity suddenly flooded Fleming.

Durrant was muttering through blood-caked lips. "The power in my head is low. It will gain momentum."

"Undoubtedly."

"Bend closer. I want to touch you."

"With death rays in your fingers?"

Durrant looked mildly surprised. He was completely rational now. "No — just touch you."

He reached out his fingers and rested them on Fleming's forehead. Fleming forced himself not to withdraw. Durrant remembered Innis and began to cry. He wished this man were his father — his lover — his enemy — his friend. He wished Fleming had killed him. He was glad he was alive.

Fleming removed his fingers. "You'll be cared for by people who care."

"Stay with me."

"I can't. You have your own strength. You don't need mine."

He went over and unbolted the door. One of the panels had been kicked out. They had believed him capable of retributive murder — even Jenny, perhaps, had believed it. He didn't blame any of them.

He spoke first to Brannigan. "Get him the coffee now." And then to Jenny, "And some water and a sponge. He needs cleaning up."

He began walking away. He couldn't look at Durrant again. He was like a dog cast out on a motorway — a rabid dog in search of a hearth. God knew what would happen to him.

Jenny caught up with him at the outside door. "You did what you had to."

"Assault and battery?"

"A promise kept."

"You heard what went on?"

"Yes. Before you bolted the door."

That an act of kindness could be brutal was a concept she had only just begun to understand.

She said, "You were strong enough to begin — and strong enough to stop."

He didn't want to talk about it any more. He said sharply, "He's bleeding. Go and see to it."

He stood in the doorway and felt the night air on his face. It was clean and sweet with the smell of summer. Jenny touched his grazed knuckles and then left him standing there. What he had done was possibly outside the law. He didn't know. He didn't care. The wounds he had inflicted on Durrant had been minimal. There was nothing to regret. He felt as if he, too, had lost blood and that the wound had been washed clean.

Twelve

DAVID WAS BURIED in a hurricane of publicity. Fleming, in the eye of the storm, saw nothing of the crowds of sightseers, the cameras, the trappings of the media. He saw David. Not David dead, he and David together in a strange unnatural silence. There were prayers, hymns, words with a mystical meaning which whispered through his mind without impact. At the grave-side he saw the coffin going down and couldn't connect David with any of it. He hadn't thought of getting a wreath. A wreath for David didn't make sense. The hearse was full of them. Great mounds of colour, expensive, pretentious. He wondered if Jenny had added a posy to the pile. If she had it was hidden by massed roses and lilies. David had owned an album of pressed flowers once, until he had decided it was cissy and had thrown it out. An interest in entomology had come next — what Ruth had called horrors in jars. A research scientist? He still hadn't cracked that one. And now never would.

Jenny, at his side, said quietly, "If we start going now while the police hold the crowds in check we can get to my car." Her eyes were tearless, but full of an almost maternal compassion for him. He, at the grave-side, was her child, her care, the one to be protected, her love. On the way down the path to the cemetery gate the cameras whirred and a reporter stepped out of line with "Just a word on your murdered son, Mr. Fleming — what are your feelings on the child's killer?"

Jenny furiously pushed him aside. She guided Fleming to the car and got him in. The car started up jerkily as if it shared her rage and shot off into the crowds, scattering them.

She didn't take him home. Nelson Street had to be kept inviolate from the Press hounds. They had bayed around The Lantern for days and he had suffered them grimly, saying little. She drove out through the town and five miles along the coast road to the old coastguard look-out. They could spend an hour or more here until the crowds dispersed. It was a place of high wide views and solitude. In the past, in moments of stress, it had brought her peace. She offered it to him now wordlessly.

He got out of the car and stood looking around him. Today the North Sea was textured like grey crepe, but with threads of silver. Marristone Port, incredibly neat at a distance, formed a geometric pattern above the harbour. The Maritime Museum with its bright and ancient craft was a point of pain which did nothing more than stab briefly at him as his eyes lingered on it. He could look with some coolness at the school half-hidden in the belt of trees. When one walked through hell one had to emerge at some stage or never emerge at all. David, in his mind not yet dead, would in time be accepted as dead. Until that happened he would talk to him in his mind. He would dismiss that cemetery down there as a nonsense. He would see this moment up here with Jenny as the only acceptable reality.

He took David's sketch of the caterpillar out of his wallet and gave it to her. "Tear it up."

She took it from him, remembering their fury with each other when she had first wanted it destroyed — fury that had turned into an act of love, violent and then tender.

Shulter's words came back to her: A mind sick with the grief of bereavement. Some day, healed, would she mean anything to him at all?

She looked down at the drawing. *Wolly Bear*. The words creased along the fold were distorted and smudged. She thought briefly of Innis. He had packed up and gone. Brannigan gave the impression he would like to go himself but was held to the school like a prisoner locked in the stocks. His near-nudity in the gym had had more dignity than pathos — something he was never likely to know, and something no-one could find the words to tell him. If the school survived, then he deserved to survive with it. He had had the courage to attend the funeral and had stood alone at the grave-side, a few paces away from the other male members of staff.

The caterpillar, mad-eyed like Durrant, leered up at her. With sharp vicious movements she tore it into small pieces and flung them into the air. The breeze caught them and scattered them.

Together they watched them go.

He thought, Peace to you, David. No more nightmares. Sleep quietly now.

Ruth had always breathed a sigh of relief at the ritual tearing up, but Jenny was still and tense.

He smiled at her. "That was always the turning point — tearing it up. Afterwards it got better."

She spoke with conviction, "And will again."

He wished the lines of strain would ease from her face. He regretted the burden of pain that he had placed on her. He loved her but couldn't find the words to say so.

He asked her abruptly if she liked Paris.

"What are you talking about?"

Life, he thought, and going onwards. But mainly I'm talking about you.

He tried telling her, clumsily and awkwardly, and her smile came slowly as she listened.

B. M. GILL

TIME AND TIME AGAIN

'She was a good friend to me – Rene. She guided me through prison like a seasoned traveller and made it bearable. We couldn't have been more different, in background, attitudes, everything. Mine was a crime of conscience – a protest demo which erupted into violence. Hers was theft. I was abject with remorse. She was annoyed at being caught. It would have been easier for everyone if the friendship had ended on the day of our release.'

But the friendship did survive. Outrage from her husband was ignored. Warnings from the police, likewise. And step by step, Maeve Barclay was led out of her safe middle-class existence into a darkening world of violence, revenge and finally murder.

'A superb new story that puts her at the pinnacle of crime fiction along with P.D. James and Ruth Rendell . . . a marvellously well-written psychological mystery'
Graham Lord, *Sunday Express*

POST A LITTLE HAPPINESS

Post·A·Book

A Royal Mail service in association with the Book Marketing Council & The Booksellers Association.

Post-A-Book is a Post Office trademark.

B. M. GILL

THE TWELFTH JUROR

Winner of the 1985 Crime Writers' Association Gold Dagger Award for the best crime novel.

On trial is Edward Carne, accused of murdering his wife. On the jury are eleven dedicated and unbiased men and women, and a twelfth, Robert Quinn, who should not be there at all.

The evidence put before the jury is tantalisingly in-conclusive, and the accused is conspicuously absent from the witness box. All this is confusing enough, but what of Robert Quinn's obsessive involvement in the trial, an obsession he will not – and indeed cannot – reveal?

'Gripping, with a chilling climax. Gill's feel for the offbeat sinister is superb'

The Times

HODDER AND STOUGHTON PAPERBACKS

MORE TITLES AVAILABLE FROM CORONET CRIME

B. M. GILL

☐	51583 X	Time and Time Again	£2.99
☐	38520 0	The Twelfth Juror	£2.50
☐	48837 9	Dying To Meet You	£2.50
☐	41341 7	Nursery Crimes	£2.50
☐	40856 1	Seminar For Murder	£2.50
☐	28112 X	Victims	£2.50

ELIZABETH FERRARS

☐	43053 2	Murder Among Friends	£2.50

PATRICIA WENTWORTH

☐	20046 4	The Case Is Closed	£2.99
☐	02714 2	Dangerpoint	£2.99
☐	10520 8	The Ivory Dagger	£2.99
☐	02715 0	The Key	£2.99

All these books are available at your local bookshop or newsagent, or can be ordered direct from the publisher. Just tick the titles you want and fill in the form below.

Prices and availability subject to change without notice.

Hodder & Stoughton Paperbacks, P.O. Box 11, Falmouth, Cornwall.

Please send cheque or postal order, and allow the following for postage and packing:

U.K. – 55p for one book, plus 22p for the second book, and 14p for each additional book ordered up to a £1.75 maximum.

B.F.P.O. and EIRE – 55p for the first book, plus 22p for the second book, and 14p per copy for the next 7 books, 8p per book thereafter.

OTHER OVERSEAS CUSTOMERS – £1.00 for the first book, plus 25p per copy for each additional book.

Name ....

Address ....

....